DUST AND ASHES

OR

DEMOLISHED.

BY
HENRYK SIENKIEWICZ,
Author of "Quo Vadis," "Children of the Soil," "Her Tragic Fate,"
"The New Soldier," "Where Worlds Meet," etc.

TRANSLATED BY
J CHRISTIAN BAY.

Fredonia Books
Amsterdam, The Netherlands

Dust and Ashes or Demolished

by
Henryk Sienkiewicz

ISBN: 1-58963-691-0

Copyright © 2002 by Fredonia Books

Reprinted from the 1899 edition

Fredonia Books
Amsterdam, The Netherlands
http://www.fredoniabooks.com

INTRODUCTION.

HENRYK SIENKIEWICZ.

I once read a short story, in which a Slav author had all the lilies and bells in a forest bending toward each other, whispering and resounding softly the words: "Glory! Glory! Glory!" until the whole forest and then the whole world repeated the song of flowers.

Such is to-day the fate of the author of the powerful historical trilogy: "With Fire and Sword," "The Deluge" and "Pan Michael," preceded by short stories, "Lillian Morris," "Yanko the Musician," "After Bread," "Hania," "Let Us Follow Him," followed by two problem novels, "Without Dogma," and "Children of the Soil," and crowned by a

5

masterpiece of an incomparable artistic beauty, "Quo Vadis." Eleven good books adopted from the Polish language and set into circulation are of great importance for the English-reading people—just now I am emphasizing only this—because these books are written in the most beautiful language ever written by any Polish author! Eleven books of masterly, personal, and simple prose! Eleven good books given to the circulation and received not only with admiration but with gratitude—books where there are more or less good or sincere pages, but where there is not one on which original humor, nobleness, charm, some comforting thoughts, some elevated sentiments do not shine. Some other author would perhaps have stopped after producing "Quo Vadis," without any doubt the best of Sienkiewicz's books. But Sienkiewicz looks into the future and cares more about works which he is

going to write, than about those which we
have already in our libraries, and he renews
his talents, searching, perhaps unknowingly,
for new themes and tendencies.

When one knows how to read a book, then
from its pages the author's face looks out on
him, a face not material, but just the same
full of life. Sienkiewicz's face, looking on us
from his books, is not always the same; it
changes, and in his last book ("Quo Vadis")
it is quite different, almost new.

There are some people who throw down a
book after having read it, as one leaves a bot-
tle after having drank the wine from it.
There are others who read books with a pencil
in their hands, and they mark the most striking passages. Afterward, in the hours of rest,
in the moments when one needs a stimulant
from within and one searches for harmony,
sympathy of a thing apparently so dead and

strange as a book is, they come back to the
marked passages, to their own thoughts, more
comprehensible since an author expressed
them; to their own sentiments, stronger and
more natural since they found them in some-
body else's words.   Because ofttimes it seems
to us—the common readers—that there is no
difference between our interior world and the
horizon of great authors, and we flatter ourselves by believing that we are only less daring, less brave than are thinkers and poets,
that some interior lack of courage stopped us
from having formulated our impressions. And
in this sentiment there is a great deal of truth.
But while this expression of our thoughts
seems to us to be a daring, to the others it is
a need; they even do not suspect how much
they are daring and new.   They must, according to the words of a poet, "Spin out the love,
as the silkworm spins its web."   That is their

capital distinction from common mortals; we recognize them by it at once; and that is the reason we put them above the common level. On the pages of their books we find not the traces of the accidental, deeper penetrating into the life or more refined feelings, but the whole harvest of thoughts, impressions, dispositions, written skilfully, because studied deeply. We also leave something on these pages. Some people dry flowers on them, the others preserve reminiscences. In every one of Sienkiewicz's volumes people will deposit a great many personal impressions, part of their souls; in every one they will find them again after many years.

There are three periods in Sienkiewicz's literary life. In the first he wrote short stories, which are masterpieces of grace and ingenuity —at least some of them. In those stories the reader will meet frequent thoughts about general problems, deep observations of life—and notwithstanding his idealism, very truthful about spiritual moods, expressed with an easy and sincere hand. Speaking about Sienkiewicz's works, no matter how small it may be, one has always the feeling that one speaks about a known, living in general memory work. Almost every one of his stories is like a stone thrown in the midst of a flock of sparrows gathering in the winter time around barns: one throw arouses at once a flock of winged reminiscences.

The other characteristics of his stories are uncommonness of his conceptions, masterly compositions, ofttimes artificial. It happens also that a story has no plot ("From the Diary of a Tutor in Pozman," "Bartek the Victor"), no action, almost no matter ("Yamyol"), but the reader is rewarded by simplicity, rural theme, humoristic pictures ("Comedy of Err-

ors: A Sketch of American Life"), pity for
the little and poor ("Yanko the Musician"),
and those qualities make the reader remember
his stories well. It is almost impossible to
forget—under the general impressions—about
his striking and standing-out figures ("The
Lighthouse Keeper of Aspinwall"), about the
individual impression they leave on our minds.
Apparently they are commonplace, every-day
people, but the author's talent puts on them an
original individuality, a particular stamp,
which makes one remember them forever and
afterward apply them to the individuals which
one meets in life. No matter how insignifi-
cant socially is the figure chosen by Sienkiewicz for his story, the great talent of the author
magnifies its striking features, not seen by
common people, and makes of it a masterpiece of literary art.

Although we have a popular saying: *Com-*

paraison n'est pas raison, one cannot refrain from stating here that this love for the poor, the little, and the oppressed, brought out so powerfully in Sienkiewicz's short stories, constitutes a link between him and François Coppée, who is so great a friend of the friendless and the oppressed, those who, without noise, bear the heaviest chains, the pariahs of our happy and smiling society. The only difference between the short stories of these two writers is this, that notwithstanding all the mastercraft of Coppée work, one forgets the impressions produced by the reading of his work—while it is almost impossible to forget "The Lighthouse Keeper" looking on any lighthouse, or "Yanko the Musician" listening to a poor wandering boy playing on the street, or "Bartek the Victor" seeing soldiers of which military discipline have made machines rather than thinking beings, or "The

Diary of a Tutor" contemplating the pale face of children overloaded with studies. Another difference between those two writers—the comparison is always between their short stories—is this, that while Sienkiewicz's figures and characters are universal, international—if one can use this adjective here—and can be applied to the students of any country, to the soldiers of any nation, to any wandering musician and to the light-keeper on any sea, the figures of François Coppée are mostly Parisian and could be hardly displaced from their Parisian surroundings and conditions.

Sometimes the whole short story is written for the sake of that which the French call *pointe*. When one has finished the reading of "Zeus's Sentence," for a moment the charming description of the evening and Athenian night is lost. And what a beautiful description it is! If the art of reading were cultivated in America as it is in France and Germany, I would not be surprised if some American Legouvé or Strakosch were to add to his répertoire such productions of prose as this humorously poetic "Zeus's Sentence," or that mystic madrigal, "Be Blessed."

"But the dusk did not last long," writes Sienkiewicz. "Soon from the Archipelago appeared the pale Selene and began to sail like a silvery boat in the heavenly space. And the walls of the Acropolis lighted again, but they beamed now with a pale green light, and looked more than ever like the vision of a dream."

But all these, and other equally charming pictures, disappear for a moment from the memory of the reader. There remains only the final joke—only Zeus's sentence. "A virtuous woman—especially when she loves another man—can resist Apollo. But surely and always a stupid woman will resist him."

Only when one thinks of the story does one see that the ending—that "immoral conclusion" I should say if I were not able to understand the joke—does not constitute the essence of the story.   Only then we find a delight in the description of the city for which the wagons cater the divine barley, and the water is carried by the girls, "with amphoræ poised on their shoulders and lifted hands, going home, light and graceful, like immortal nymphs."

And then follow such paragraphs as the following which determine the real value of the work:

"The voice of the God of Poetry sounded so beautiful that it performed a miracle. Behold!   In the Ambrosian night the gold spear standing on the Acropolis of Athens trembled, and the marble head of the gigantic statue turned toward the Acropolis in order to hear better. . . . Heaven and earth listened to it; the sea stopped roaring and lay peacefully near the shores; even pale Selene stopped her night wandering in the sky and stood motionless over Athens."

"And when Apollo had finished, a light wind arose and carried the song through the whole of Greece, and wherever a child in the cradle heard only a tone of it, that child grew into a poet."

What poet? Famed by what song? Will he not perhaps be a lyric poet?

The same happens with "Lux in Tenebris." One reads again and again the description of the fall of the mist and the splashing of the rain dropping in the gutter, "the cawing of the crows, migrating to the city for their winter quarters, and, with flapping of wings, roosting in the trees." One feels that the whole misery of the first ten pages was necessary in order to form a background for the two pages of heavenly light, to bring out the brightness of that light. "Those who have lost their best beloved," writes Sienkiewicz, "must hang their lives on something; otherwise they could not exist." In such sentences —and it is not the prettiest, but the shortest that I have quoted—resounds, however, the quieting wisdom, the noble love of that art which poor Kamionka "respected deeply and was always sincere toward." During the long years of his profession he never cheated nor wronged it, neither for the sake of fame nor money, nor for praise nor for criticism. He always wrote as he felt. Were I not like Ruth of the Bible, doomed to pick the ears of corn instead of being myself a sower—if God had not made me critic and worshipper but artist and creator—I could not wish for another ne-

2

crology than those words of Sienkiewicz regarding the statuary Kamionka.

Quite another thing is the story "At the
Source." None of the stories except "Let Us
Follow Him" possess for me so many tran-
scendent beauties, although we are right to be
angry with the author for having wished, during the reading of several pages, to make us
believe an impossible thing—that he was de-
ceiving us. It is true that he has done it in a
masterly manner—it is true that he could not
have done otherwise, but at the same time
there is a fault in the conception, and although
Sienkiewicz has covered the precipice with
flowers, nevertheless the precipice exists.

On the other hand, it is true that one reading the novel will forget the trick of the author
and will see in it only the picture of an immense happiness and a hymn in the worship of
love. Perhaps the poor student is right when

he says: "Among all the sources of happiness, that from which I drank during the fever is the clearest and best." "A life which love has not visited, even in a dream, is still worse."

Love and faith in woman and art are two constantly recurring themes in "Lux in Tenebris," "At the Source," "Be Blessed," and "Organist of Ponikila."

When Sienkiewicz wrote "Let Us Follow Him," some critics cried angrily that he lessens his talent and moral worth of the literature; they regretted that he turned people into the false road of mysticism, long since left. Having found Christ on his pages, the least religious people have recollected how gigantic he is in the writings of Heine, walking over land and sea, carrying a red, burning sun instead of a heart. They all understood that to introduce Christ not only worthily or beautifully, but simply and in such a manner that we would not be obliged to turn away from the picture, would be a great art—almost a triumph.

In later times we have made many such attempts. "The Mysticism" became to-day an article of commerce. The religious tenderness and simplicity was spread among Parisian newspaper men, playwrights and novelists. Such as Armand Sylvèstre, such as Theodore de Wyzewa, are playing at writing up Christian dogmas and legends. And a strange thing! While the painters try to bring the Christ nearer to the crowd, while Fritz von Uhde or Lhermitte put the Christ in a country school, in a workingman's house, the weakling writers, imitating poets, dress Him in old, faded, traditional clothes and surround Him with a theatrical light which they dare to call "mysticism." They are crowding the porticos of the temple, but they are merely merchants.   Anatole France alone cannot be placed in the same crowd.

In "Let Us Follow Him" the situation and characters are known, and are already to be found in literature.   But never were they painted so simply, so modestly, without romantic complaints and exclamations.   In the first chapters of that story there appears an epic writer with whom we have for a long time been familiar.   We are accustomed to that uncommon simplicity.   But in order to appreciate the narrative regarding Antea, one must listen attentively to this slow prose and then one will notice the rhythmic sentences following one after the other.   Then one feels that the author is building a great foundation for the action. Sometimes there occurs a brief, sharp sentence ending in a strong, short word, and the result is that Sienkiewicz has given us a masterpiece which justifies the enthusiasm of a critic, who called him a Prince of Polish Prose.

In the second period of his literary activity, Sienkiewicz has produced his remarkable historical trilogy, "The Deluge," "With Fire and Sword," and "Pan Michael," in which his talent shines forth powerfully, and which possess absolutely distinctive characters from his short stories. The admirers of romanticism cannot find any better books in historical fiction. Some critic has said righteously about Sienkiewicz, speaking of his "Deluge," that he is "the first of Polish novelists, past or present, and second to none now living in England, France, or Germany."

Sienkiewicz being himself a nobleman, therefore naturally in his historical novels he describes the glorious deeds of the Polish nobility, who, being located on the frontier of such barbarous nations as Turks, Kozaks,

Tartars, and Wolochs (to-day Roumania), had defended Europe for centuries from the invasions of barbarism and gave the time to Germany, France, and England to outstrip Poland in the development of material welfare and general civilization among the masses—the nobility being always very refined—though in the fifteenth century the literature of Poland and her sister Bohemia (Chechy) was richer than any other European country, except Italy. One should at least always remember that Nicolaus Kopernicus (Kopernik) was a Pole and John Huss was a Chech.

Historical novels began in England, or rather in Scotland, by the genius of Walter Scott, followed in France by Alexandre Dumas *pere*. These two great writers had numerous followers and imitators in all countries, and every nation can point out some more or less successful writer in that field, but who

never attained the great success of Sienkiewicz, whose works are translated into many
languages, even into Russian, where the antipathy for the Polish superior degree of civilization is still very eager.

The superiority of Sienkiewicz's talent is
then affirmed by this fact of translation, and I
would dare say that he is superior to the father
of this kind of novels, on account of his historical coloring, so much emphasized in Walter Scott. This important quality in the historical novel is truer and more lively in the
Polish writer, and then he possesses that psychological depth about which Walter Scott
never dreamed. Walter Scott never has created such an original and typical figure as Za-
globa is, who is a worthy rival to Shakespeare's Falstaff. As for the description of
duelings, fights, battles, Sienkiewicz's fantas-
tically heroic pen is without rival.

Alexandre Dumas, notwithstanding the biting criticism of Brunetière, will always remain a great favorite with the reading masses, who are searching in his books for pleasure, amusement, and distraction. Sienkiewicz's historical novels possess all the interesting qualities of Dumas, and besides that they are full of wholesome food for thinking minds. His colors are more shining, his brush is broader, his composition more artful, chiselled, finished, better built, and executed with more vigor. While Dumas amuses, pleases, distracts, Sienkiewicz astonishes, surprises, bewitches. All uneasy preoccupations, the dolorous echoes of eternal problems, which philosophical doubt imposes with the everlasting anguish of the human mind, the mystery of the origin, the enigma of destiny, the inexplicable necessity of suffering, the short, tragical, and sublime vision of the future of the soul, and the future not less difficult to be guessed of by the human race in this material world, the torments of human conscience and responsibility for the deeds, is said by Sienkiewicz without any pedanticism, without any dryness.

If we say that the great Hungarian author Maurice Jokai, who also writes historical novels, pales when compared with that fascinating Pole who leaves far behind him the late lions in the field of romanticism, Stanley J. Weyman and Anthony Hope, we are through with that part of Sienkiewicz's literary achievements.

In the third period Sienkiewicz is represented by two problem novels, "Without Dogma" and "Children of the Soil."

The charm of Sienkiewicz's psychological novels is the synthesis so seldom realized and as I have already said, the plastic beauty and abstract thoughts. He possesses also an ad-

mirable assurance of psychological analysis, a
mastery in the painting of customs and characters, and the rarest and most precious faculty of animating his heroes with intense, personal life, which, though it is only an illusion-
ary life appears less deceitful than the real
life.

In that field of novels Sienkiewicz differs
greatly from Balzac, for instance, who forced
himself to paint the man in his perversity or in
his stupidity. According to his views life is
the racing after riches. The whole of Balzac's
philosophy can be resumed in the deification
of the force. All his heroes are "strong men"
who disdain humanity and take advantage of
it. Sienkiewicz's psychological novels are not
lacking in the ideal in his conception of life;
they are active powers, forming human souls.
The reader finds there, in a well-balanced proportion, good and bad ideas of life, and he rep-

resents this life as a good thing, worthy of living.

He differs also from Paul Bourget, who as a German savant counts how many microbes are in a drop of spoiled blood, who is pleased with any ferment, who does not care for healthy souls, as a doctor does not care for healthy people—and who is fond of corruption. Sienkiewicz's analysis of life is not exclusively pathological, and we find in his novels healthy as well as sick people as in the real life. He takes colors from twilight and aurora to paint with, and by doing so he strengthens our energy, he stimulates our ability for thinking about those eternal problems, difficult to be decided, but which existed and will exist as long as humanity will exist.

He prefers green fields, the perfume of flowers, health, virtue, to Zola's liking for crime, sickness, cadaverous putridness, and manure.

He prefers *l' ame humaine* to *la bete humaine*.

He is never vulgar even when his heroes do not wear any gloves, and he has these common points with Shakespeare and Molière, that he does not paint only certain types of humanity, taken from one certain part of the country, as it is with the majority of French writers who do not go out of their dear Paris; in Sienkiewicz's novels one can find every kind of people, beginning with humble peasants and modest noblemen created by God, and ending with proud lords made by the kings.

In the novel "Without Dogma," there are many keen and sharp observations, said masterly and briefly; there are many states of the soul, if not always very deep, at least written with art.   And his merit in that respect is greater than of any other writers, if we take in consideration that in Poland heroic lyricism and poetical picturesqueness prevail in the literature.

The one who wishes to find in the modern literature some aphorism to classify the characteristics of the people, in order to be able afterward to apply them to their fellow-men, must read "Children of the Soil."

But the one who is less selfish and wicked, and wishes to collect for his own use such a library as to be able at any moment to take a book from a shelf and find in it something which would make him thoughtful or would make him forget the ordinary life,—he must get "Quo Vadis," because there he will find pages which will recomfort him by their beauty and dignity; it will enable him to go out from his surroundings and enter into himself, *i. e.*, in that better man whom we sometimes feel in our interior. And while reading this book he ought to leave on its pages the traces of his readings, some marks made with a lead pencil or with his whole memory.

It seems that in that book a new man was aroused in Sienkiewicz, and any praise said about this unrivaled masterpiece will be as pale as any powerful lamp is pale comparatively with the glory of the sun. For instance. if I say that Sienkiewicz has made a thorough study of Nero's epoch, and that his great talent and his plastic imagination created the most powerful pictures in the historical background, will it not be a very tame praise, compared with his book—which, while reading it, one shivers and the blood freezes in one's veins?

In "Quo Vadis" the whole *alta Roma*, beginning with slaves carrying mosaics for their refined masters, and ending with patricians, who were so fond of beautiful things that one of them for instance used to kiss at every mo-

ment a superb vase, stands before our eyes as
if it was reconstructed by a magical power
from ruins and death.

There is no better description of the burning of Rome in any literature. While reading
it everything turns red in one's eyes, and immense noises fill one's ears. And the moment
when Christ appears on the hill to the frightened Peter, who is going to leave Rome, not
feeling strong enough to fight with mighty
Cæsar, will remain one of the strongest passages of the literature of the whole world.

After having read again and again this
great—shall I say the greatest historical novel?—and having wondered at its deep conception, masterly execution, beautiful language,
powerful painting of the epoch, plastic description of customs and habits, enthusiasm of
the first followers of Christ, refinement of Roman civilization, corruption of the old world,

the question rises: What is the dominating idea of the author, spread out all over the whole book?   It is the cry of Christians murdered in circuses: *Pro Christo!*

Sienkiewicz searching always and continually for a tranquil harbor from the storms of conscience and investigation of the tormented mind, finds such a harbor in the religious sentiments, in lively Christian faith.   This idea is woven as golden thread in a silk brocade, not only in "Quo Vadis," but also in all his novels. In "Fire and Sword" his principal hero is an outlaw; but all his crimes, not only against society, but also against nature, are redeemed by faith, and as a consequence of it afterward by good deeds.   In the "Children of the Soul," he takes one of his principal characters upon one of seven Roman hills, and having displayed before him in the most eloquent way the might of the old Rome, the might as it

3

never existed before and perhaps never will exist again, he says: "And from all that nothing is left only crosses! crosses! crosses!" It seems to us that in "Quo Vadis" Sienkiewicz strained all his forces to reproduce from one side all the power, all riches, all refinement, all corruption of the Roman civilization in order to get a better contrast with the great advantages of the cry of the living faith: *Pro Christo!* In that cry the asphyxiated not only in old times but in our days also find refreshment; the tormented by doubt, peace. From that cry flows hope, and naturally people prefer those from whom the blessing comes to those who curse and doom them.

Sienkiewicz considers the Christian faith as the principal and even the only help which humanity needs to bear cheerfully the burden and struggle of every-day life. Equally his personal experience as well as his studies made him worship Christ. He is not one of those who say that religion is good for the people at large. He does not admit such a shade of contempt in a question touching so near the human heart. He knows that every one is a man in the presence of sorrow and the conundrum of fate, contradiction of justice, tearing of death, and uneasiness of hope. He believes that the only way to cross the precipice is the flight with the wings of faith, the precipice made between the submission to general and absolute laws and the confidence in the infinite goodness of the Father.

The time passes and carries with it people and doctrines and systems. Many authors left as the heritage to civilization rows of books, and in those books scepticism, indifference, doubt, lack of precision and decision.

But the last symptoms in the literature show us that the Stoicism is not sufficient for our

generation, not satisfied with Marcus Aurel-
ius's gospel, which was not sufficient even to
that brilliant Sienkiewicz's Roman *arbiter ele-
gantiarum*, the over-refined patrician Petron-
ius.   A nation which desired to live, and does
not wish either to perish in the desert or be
drowned in the mud, needs such a great help
which only religion gives.   The history is not
only *magister vitae*, but also it is the master of
conscience.

Literature has in Sienkiewicz a great poet—
epical as well as lyrical.

I shall not mourn, although I appreciate the
justified complaint about objectivity in *belles
lettres*.   But now there is no question what
poetry will be; there is the question whether
it will be, and I believe that society, being
tired with Zola's realism and its caricature, not
with the picturesqueness of Loti, but with
catalogues of painter's colors; not with the

depth of Ibsen, but the oddness of his imitators—it seems to me that society will hate the poetry which discusses and philosophizes, wishes to paint but does not feel, makes archeology but does not give impressions, and that people will turn to the poetry as it was in the beginning, what is in its deepest essence, to the flight of single words, to the interior melody, to the song—the art of sounds being the greatest art. I believe that if in the future the poetry will find listeners, they will repeat to the poets the words of Paul Verlaine, whom by too summary judgment they count among incomprehensible originals:

"De la musique encore et toujours."

And nobody need be afraid from a social point of view, for Sienkiewicz's objectivity. It is a manly lyricism as well as epic, made deep by the knowledge of the life, sustained

by thinking, until now perhaps unconscious
of itself, the poetry of a writer who walked
many roads, studied many things, knew much
bitterness, ridiculed many triflings, and then
he perceived that a man like himself has only
one aim: above human affairs "to spin the
love, as the silkworm spins its web."

S. C. DE SOISSONS.

"The University," Cambridge, Mass.

DUST AND ASHES

DUST AND ASHES.

CHAPTER I.

"Well, we have reached Kiew."

The speaker, young Joseph Schwarz, had been suddenly roused from a reverie, as the vehicle in which he was seated became subject to certain formalities, on passing the public gates of the ancient city. He glanced around, pleased with the long-expected revelation of town-made dwellings, the sight of which made his heart expand with joy:—Young and happy, he drew a long breath, filling both of his broad, healthy lungs with air, and repeating, in a tone of genuine satisfaction:

"Well, we have reached Kiew."

The Jewish "budka" was jolting slowly along the paved streets. Schwarz, growing

tired of remaining under the canvas of the
vehicle, alighted and bid the driver stop at
some neighboring inn, whereupon he took to
the sidewalk, keeping the budka in sight. As
usual, the crowds in the streets passed to and
fro; shop windows paraded with sparkling ex-
hibitions; carriages of all descriptions wound
their way along the thoroughfares, and the
figures of by-passing merchants, soldiers, beg-
gars and monks met the wondering gaze of
the young newcomer.

It was market-day, so the city had assumed
an aspect characteristic of such gatherings;—
no movement, or word, or gesture, was likely
to be lost in the crowd. The tradesman
minded his business; the officer observed his
duties; the rascal attended to his fraudulent
transactions: Everybody aimed at some
definite end, and everyone had his individual
object in view, thinking of the morrow, hop-
ing and planning; and amidst pushing and
pulling the burning hot atmosphere hovered
over the city, while the sun was reflected

equally gloriously by palace windows and by the panes of shop windows.

"What a noise," thought Schwarz, who had never before visited a large city. "This is life, indeed!"

He began reflecting upon the wide difference between the narrowly circumscribed village life and the great possibilities of the city, when a well-known voice reached his ears:

"Faith!—Joseph!"

Schwarz turned about and found himself face to face with the person who had addressed him by name. He scanned the man's face narrowly, but at last extended his arms, exclaiming:

"Faith!—Gustave!"

Gustave was a slim youth of about twenty-three, whose chestnut colored hair, reaching down almost as far as his shoulders, made him appear older than he really was. So did also the reddish, cropped beard.

"How do you do, Joseph? What are you

doing here?—Attending lectures at the University, eh?"

"That is my intention."

"Right!" said his friend. "Life is miserable in the absence of knowledge.—What course do you intend to follow?"

"I don't know as yet," replied Schwarz. "One must needs become familiar with the different courses before deciding."

"To be sure. By all means take time and consider. I am here already a year and took ample time to make my choice. I regret my decision, however,—but then, it's too late to think of a change, although I scarcely know how to proceed. Weakness, probably! It is easier to make a blunder than to set matters right again.—Well, to-morrow I'll take you over to the University, and in the meantime you may have your baggage brought to my quarters, unless you've already secured a room. I am living close by, so you may start in chumming with me, and when you grow

tired of that, another companion may be selected for you."

Schwarz accepted Gustave's proposition,
and in a short while the two found themselves
in a diminutive den,—a "study."

"Well," said Gustave, seeking with his eyes
a convenient space for his friend's small trunk
and sundry belongings, "we've been parted a
good long time,—one whole year, I daresay.
What have you been doing all this time?"

"Staying with my father. He rather dis-
liked my idea of going to the University."

"What harm could it do him?"

"He was an honest, but simple man;—a
blacksmith, you know."

"Why did he consent now?"

"He died."

"Oh, yes—," returned Gustave, with a
cough.—"Why, that confounded asthma has
troubled me for very nearly six months. You
wonder, I suppose, at my sniffing, but only
wait till you begin poring over the books, as
I am doing, without resting day or night.—

And then go about and fight for your bread
and butter, like dogs fight one another;—
have you money?"

"Certainly. I turned into money all that
was left by my father. There are two thousand rubles to my credit."

"Two thousand!—That'll be sufficient.—
Well, I am troubled, as I said, with that confounded asthma,—and yet, one is obliged to
stick to his books. In fact, in the evening I
hardly ever find time to draw a breath of
fresh air, and the lectures extend over the
livelong day. It is impossible to get enough
of sleep.—Such is our way of living, and as
soon as you become familiar with the true
state of things in this place you'll begin to
comprehend what a university means. To-
night I'll take upon myself to introducing
you in our club, or, rather, at our official term,
in order that you may at once become acquainted with your future comrades."

While talking in this strain, Gustave busied
himself with the comfort of his guest and went

about the room, sniffing and coughing. His
curved back, his thin face and long hair sug-
gested that the weakness of which he complained was due rather to the pursuit of pleasure than to ardent study. The crowded book-
cases and other literary material; the general
air of poverty about the room indicated, however, that Gustave belonged to the class of
night-birds that lose one feather after another
over the books, and expire their last breath
over some accentuated or unaccentuated letter. Still, Schwarz assimilated, with a feeling
of genuine satisfaction, the atmosphere of the
little room, which revealed to him a new, yet
strangely isolated world.—"Who knows,"
thought he, "what great thoughts may be fostered among such garret philosophers? Who
knows what a future such dreary dens may
keep in store for science?"

"You will become acquainted with a great
many of our friends and comrades to-night,"
said Gustave, pulling forth from under the
bedstead a small tea-kitchen and supporting

its one broken edge by means of a fragment of a flower-pot. "It will be well for you not to assume an attitude of opposition to our club," continued he—"I'll just prepare a cup of tea—and even the most ridiculous fellows should not make you shun the place. When you become familiar with the city and its population, you'll realize there is no want of blockheads, while we are justly proud, on the other hand, of a number of quite distinguished men with whom you will easily form acquaintance. On the whole, it will be of some importance to you to find out the state of affairs for yourself. Our mode of living is somewhat artificial, somewhat strange and ridiculous, but again, our progress is by no means slow. Original characters are not rare among us, nor is our brotherhood devoid of blank minds, of emptiness, of puffed-up stupidity. In some brains the spirit burns clear and bright; in others there is perfect darkness."

A pause ensued which was broken only by

Gustave's broken cough and his blowing at the embers in the tea-kitchen. Twilight set in, and the shadows on the walls and the floor of the study grew darker and darker. The narrow halo surrounding the student's cooking apparatus rose and fell, until at length the kettle began to sing, and proceeded to seeth and snort. Gustave lighted a candle.

"There, drink a cup of tea while I go out to give a lesson. Wait for me here, or throw yourself on the bed and take a nap, if you grow tired. Giving lessons you will learn soon enough,—when your money gives out, if not earlier. It is a tedious matter, but there is no alternative. A student's life has many drawbacks,—yet why speak of them! Our sphere is entirely different from the remainder of the world. We are not loved by the general public; nobody thinks of extending invitations to our circles;—we are at war with society and even with one another, — — hard enough in many ways! If you happen to fall sick, no one will reach out his hand to help

4

you, unless some friend and comrade knows how you are situated. Well, most of our surroundings are displeased with our habit of naming everything by its proper name;—they oppose us, because we refuse to wear masks before the world."

"Your views are rather pessimistic," ventured Schwarz.

"Pessimistic or otherwise," interrupted Gustave bitterly, "you will find out for yourself. I merely promise you will not sleep on roses. Youth has her rights, her privileges. When you attempt urging them, they laugh at you; they speak of you as a person who has no right of fostering ideas; they call your thoughts fantastical. Yet, let them call them whatever they please,—when the heart burns and aches,—ah, you will feel it soon enough! — — — Take a cup of tea and rest yourself. In one hour I'll join you. Good-bye."

For a moment Schwarz sat listening to the steps of his friend, until the sound was drowned in the rush outside, and he realized that he was alone.   Gustave's words had made a singular impression upon him.   Joseph's former recollections of his friend bore an aspect entirely different from the impression he had just received. The voice that greeted him on his arrival at the city was not free from a strain of censoriousness and disgust, and his morose disposition expressed itself in partly violent, partly sad words.   Formerly sound in body and mind, he was now breathing heavily, and both his speech and his movements bore witness of a singular mental excitement, as though his spiritual powers were on the point of becoming exhausted.

"Can this really be the outcome of his struggle for life?" thought Schwarz. "Then, attending the University means struggling, going against the current, and the poor fellows seem to lack the necessary power! Why, they are bound to win, somehow or other, in spite of the opposition! Of course, it is not play-work, yet Gustave is too much of a misanthropist. Probably he has burned his feathers and received some permanent injury. Still, the room bears ample witness of the studious habits of its inhabitant, consequently he is progressing. And who knows if his misanthropic mien is not an artificial cover under which he may pursue his plans and proceed with more safety. But suppose it really should prove necessary to bury one's self in such a mass of revolutionary truck, —— well, I'll do it, and even place myself at the head," cried the young man energetically.

About an hour after this soliloquy a sniffing was heard at the staircase, whereupon Gustave opened the door and walked, or rather pushed, himself through the opening.

"Now let us be off," exclaimed he. "You are now facing the whirlpool of a student's life, and to-night you shall see the agreeable features of the maelstrom. There is no time to be lost."

He glanced critically at his cap, scanned the room from one end to another and stepped over to a table. from the draw of which he drew forth a comb and began passing it through his long, brown hair, which was already marked by a few grayish stains. At length they went out into the streets. In those days Kiew possessed some genuine students' inns. The public spirit was of such a nature that the young men who attended University courses were prohibited from moving in the social circles. The different cliques of the city viewed the young element with anything but friendly feelings, although the latter might well be extended to those who struggled for the purpose of getting a foothold in the world outside. But the young men's disregard of conventional laws; their violent words and manners, and other characteristics of youth were not adapted to the established rules of society; thus the University became surrounded by an exclusive body, which moved about its books and its clubs and its private interests day by day. For many different reasons this condition of affairs was equally good and bad, for when the young men were at length ready to face the world about them, they bore a decided aspect of readiness and alacrity; there were no tired or bored spirits among them.

The two men crossed the street and walked rapidly toward a building that was clearly outlined by rows of lighted windows. This was the club-house. The moonlight falling over the figures of Joseph and his companion produced two strangely different shadows: the broad, strong figure of Schwarz and the thin, stooping frame of Gustave, with its large head. Gustave led the way, sometimes addressing Joseph, sometimes stopping to hold a monologue, until their destination was reached, and he drew himself up, whereupon he, catching hold of the cornice and lifting himself up, commenced scanning the interior of the public-room through the window. At length he loosened his hold of the cornice, wiped the dust from his knees and exclaimed:

"Not there."

"Who?"

"May have been there, or may have left for good."

"Whom do you speak of?"

"What's the time?"

"Past ten o'clock. Were you looking for anyone in particular?"

"Yes. The widow."

"A widow? Who is she?"

"I'm afraid she is ill."

"Some acquaintance of yours?"

"Of course. Unless I knew her there would be no reason in my taking any interest in her."

"Certainly not," returned Schwarz. "Well, let us walk in."

He turned the handle of the door, and they found themselves in the hall of the public-house. A hot, smoky atmosphere at once enshrouded the two men. Faces of different age and expression met their glance from the different corners of the room; they were nearly all strange to Schwarz. The monotonous strain of piano music accompanied by a guitar

penetrated the clouds of smoke and was sometimes deafened by roars of laughter from the
crowd. The guitar was played by a tall,
young man of haggard appearance and with
close-cropped hair and a scar on his face. His
long fingers moved listlessly across the strings,
while his large, blue eyes were meditatively
fixed on the edge of the platform. The pianist might hardly be said to have passed the
years of childhood; his delicate teint and long
hair gave him a somewhat sickly appearance.
There was a graceful trait about his mouth and
spite in his eyes. The red spots on his cheeks
and his whole bearing indicated that he had
been playing long and was exhausted. Several tall, strong-looking young men had surrounded the players; their attitudes and their
changing expressions of countenance gave
evidence of the great attention with which
they were listening. Others were seated on
chairs and benches, and young ladies of the
grasshopper types were active here and there.
A confused noise issued from all corners, gen-

erally intermixed with the clank of mugs and glassware. In the alcoves adjoining the main hall card-playing took place at a furious rate; through a half open door the countenance of one of the players became plainly visible, as he lighted his cigar by a candle, the momentarily rising and falling flame of which, illuminated his haggard features. The lady cashier at the desk viewed the scene with perfect equanimity from behind the quill-pen with which she made her daily entries; next to her a young girl, her assistant, was soundly asleep, sitting on a chair and preserving her equilibrium in a wonderful manner. A big cat was perched at the corner of a table and maintained, alternately opening and closing her eyes, an inviolable expression of dignity and philosophical calm. Schwarz glanced around the crowd.

"Hallo, there, Schwarz, how do you do?" cried several voices.

"Well enough. Good evening."

"Going to stay with us?"

"Certainly."

"I desire to introduce him to our honorable society as a new member. You had better learn at once, however, that your obligation to appear on these premises every day embodies the privilege of never enjoying your full measure of sleep," interposed Gustave.

"A member," repeated some one. "So much the better. Let's have a speech. Hallo, Augustinowicz, let's hear from you!"

A young man, stooping, and with a bald head, entered the room. Throwing his soiled cap on the table he ascended a chair and began as follows:

"Gentlemen, unless you remain quiet I shall trouble myself to make a learned oration before your assemblage. I am aware, gentlemen and friends, that nothing is more apt to throw you into confusion than erudite speaking. By Jupiter, why can you never accommodate yourselves to parliamentary proceedings?—Quiet! What, a noise;—quiet, I say, unless you want me to make a learned oration!"

The threat produced a momentary hush, and the speaker, glancing about triumphantly, proceeded:

"Gentlemen, when we assemble here it is not for the purpose of seeking quietude in order to forget the unpleasant moments in our lives (Very good!). As a daily visitor here I know this to be absolutely true (Very good!). You cannot deny the presence of myself,—you cannot deny my presence here to-night (Applause; the speaker is highly gratified). Quiet! But as I become aware that all my efforts toward establishing a definite purpose of our society are wrecked on the general fickleness among you,—for it is general among us (Certainly, certainly!);—when I see how they are never promoted, as they should be, by a universal concord on your part; that such concord is frustrated in its very process of being—I beg you note: While it is being formed among us,—frustrated, as are the attempts of the few promoters thereof;—when the isolated attempts of perfecting a definite purpose in our society never become united into an organic purpose, a oneness; when they never leave the province of dreaming and enter the field of realistic activity,—then, gentlemen, I am prepared, and so are others, to call forth a revolution of our unity, of the present manner in which we conduct our affairs (Clapping of hands); then I am prepared to employ other means (Certainly, certainly!) that will appeal to the few if not to the multitude." (Boisterous applause.)

"What does this mean?" asked Schwarz.

Gustave shrugged his shoulders.

"A speech."

"For what purpose?"

"Who cares to know!"

"Well, what does it all signify?"

"His name is Augustinowicz, a good fellow, but drunk at present, so his thoughts are obscured. Otherwise he knows what he will, and I declare he is right."

"What are his ideas?"

"That we should not assemble here in vain, but with a definite end in view. They laugh at the purpose, however, as well as of the speech. Of course the realization of such an idea would collide with the so-called liberty and indolence that has hitherto governed our society."

"What purpose does Augustinowicz favor?"

"A literary, a scientific one."

"Why, then he seems to be right."

"I told you he was right. If some one else had made the same motion, probably it would have been carried."

"Well, and he?"

"All that he touches will bear marks of his own ridiculous and degraded individuality. Beware, Schwarz; so far as I know you, you have nothing in common with him. In this place every one is in danger of stumbling one way or another."

Gustave fixed his glance on Augustinowicz, shrugged his shoulders and continued:

"This man is quite singular in all respects. I tell you, he is an aggregate of all possible abilities in a low character; of exalted ideas and bad acts—an eternal lack of harmony. He is never able to reach the correct proportion of purpose and actual capability, and therefore his life is demolished."

In the meantime Schwarz discovered several young men of his acquaintance, and a general chatting ensued over the glasses, during which Schwarz obtained some information regarding the University.

"Do you all have intercourse with one another?"

"That is impossible," replied one of the Lithuanians. "Persons of radically different ideas are coming here to pursue their studies, and consequently there are many different coteries."

"Is that not a disadvantage?"

"Not exactly. Unity in certain general matters is very well, but unity in collegiate life is an impossibility. It would lead to nothing, even if attempted."

"How about German universities?"

"There, too, are associations and societies that pursue a purpose of their own. At any rate, among us the ideas must necessarily correspond with the practical life of each individual student, as difference in the one respect is accompanied by a difference in the other."

"Then, you really form no unions?"

"That is another matter: We unite about our University interests, or other affairs of general importance concerning everybody. Whatever you may find pointing in the opposite direction will be proofs, I think, of our vital powers: It will testify that we live, feel and think. There is our unity: What separates us tends to unite us."

"What is your common ensign?"

"Working and suffering. We do not invent names for our societies; the Farmers' Friends name us Bakers' Boys."

"Indeed?"

"Certainly. Experience will teach you the significance of the name. We all are anxious to secure rooms in houses inhabited by bakers; to become acquainted with the respective bakers and gain credit with them. This is a great help to us, as we are generally trusted. The majority of us never get a warm meal, but dry bread on credit you can obtain as long as you care for it."

"Fine prospects, indeed."

"Fine, indeed! Besides our coterie which has adopted no definite name there is one called the Farmers' Friends; it was founded and fostered by Augustinowicz, and Rylski and Antoniewicz have the lead at present. They are fools who do not know their own purpose: They speak Little Russian and drink fusel, that's all."

"What other organizations are there?"

"Really none. Still, there are many apologies for such. One combines common scientific interests, others unite certain social claims. You will meet aristocrats, democrats,

ultramontanists and liberals, even drunkards,
fools, good-for-nothings and fanatical laborers
in the different organizations."

"Who is considered the most promising
student?"

"The best student?"

"Yes."

"That is according to their special studies.
Some say that Augustinowicz knows a great
deal—not thoroughly, however. But so far
as conscientious study—and that is, of course,
the main consideration—Gustave surpasses all
others."

"Is that so?"

"He is subject of considerable discussion at
present. Some dislike his manners, but as
you will occupy the same room as he you may
judge for yourself. For instance, his affair
with the widow,—well, it's sheer over-excite-
ment, and nothing else; another would choose
a different course. It's true, however, that
the matter is by no means an easy one."

"I heard Gustave speaking of her. Who may she be?"

"She is a young lady whom we all know. Her fate is quite sad. She fell in love with Potkansky, the lawyer,—all fire and flame, it is said. I don't recollect those times, but I remember Potkansky quite well. He was a young man of excellent abilities, immensely wealthy and assiduous in his studies, and counted a sort of demigod by the whole brotherhood. I don't know how he made the woman's acquaintance,—the story is told differently—but so much is sure: They were over heads and ears in love with each other, and she was but eighteen years old. At length Potkansky decided upon marrying her. There was no end of opposition in his family, but Potkansky had decided to take the step,—he was all alive with energy, and so they were married in spite of all attempts to prevent this step. They lived together a year, when he died suddenly of typhus, without provisions for her future, as the family at once seized up-

on his property. Their only child died soon
after; then she was all alone and would have
become utterly ruined, unless Gustave had appeared on the scene."

"What did Gustave do?"

"I declare he did wonderful things.   In
spite of his limited means he filed suit against
the Potkansky family, and heaven knows
whether he'd ever have won it, for it is a family of magnates.   Still, his efforts were successful inasmuch as they consented to pay a
small annual pension to the widow during her
natural life."

"He is quite energetical, then!"

"All full of energy,—a great fellow, I tell
you.   Only think, he was but one year at the
University, and had very few acquaintances,
no means,—no money. Still, that's the way
it goes, my friend: Rich people can gain their
rights; the poor classes enforce their rights."

"What claims had she on him?"

"He was Potkansky's friend; but—well, that
is not sufficient to make you understand. The

fact is that he loved her even before she became the wife of Potkansky,—kept himself out of their way. At present he makes no secret of his feelings."

"And she?"

"Oh, she has become more and more eccentric, since her troubles began. Now she is simply insane, and does not realize what happens to her,—insensible to everything. You will no doubt see a great deal of her, as she appears here every day."

"How so?"

"Well, her mind is deranged, as I said. It is generally supposed that she saw Potkansky the first time in these rooms. However that may be, she can't realize that he is dead, therefore she is seeking him everywhere. Of course, if he returned to this world he would be found here sure enough. Yea, maybe we'll call him back some day; they received a great many of us in their house."

"And Gustave permits her to come here?"

"Potkansky would never have allowed her,

—but with Gustave the case is quite different."

"How does she treat him?"

"Like a piece of furniture, a plate, or a ball of thread. She does not appear to pay the least attention to him, but she does not avoid him. I believe it goes hard with the poor fellow; still, that's his own affair. Well, there she is, —there, to the right of the entrance."

As the widow entered the room the noise subsided to a certain extent. The appearance of the mysterious-looking figure always produced a feeling of awe in the company. She was rather above middle height, with an oval face, light hair and dark eyes, and a perfect virginal form. Earnestness and sorrow had produced plainly visible marks on her high, white forehead. The deep shadows under her eyes and the finely arched eyebrows made the eyes appear as though they were shaded from all sides. The expression of the eyes was remarkable: The color and lustre of polished steel seemed to emanate from them as well as to be reflected by them,—a light and nothing else; the lustre seemed deprived of both warmth and intelligence. They looked, but saw nothing; they did not receive the pictures of the objects, but merely reflected them. They called forth a feeling indescribably cold, and as the eyelids never seemed to move and the pupils maintained a regular searching and hunting, peering kind of motion, the impression was almost awe-inspiring. Her features corresponded in every way to this effect. The lips were curved downward like those of a statue, and her skin bore a brownish hue. She was neither pretty nor winning, but merely perfectly beautiful. This, however, did not make her less attractive; it lent her a certain irresistible charm and made one feel that even if she bore the unqualified appearance of a statue, she was a woman of flesh and blood. In fact, she was equally attractive and repulsive, and Gustave felt it keener than any one else. Her calm and rigid bearing puzzled him, it seemed, as though his inclinations toward her were prompted by no life, or cause in herself. Her symbol might be a sleeping flower; indeed, suffering and sorrow had produced her vacancy of mind and soul. The close of her short career of happiness was marked by two coffins. During maidenhood she had experienced what love is, but the object of her love was no more. A mother's love had awakened still deeper feelings in her heart,—her child was dead. Henceforth she lived, herself, no more, she merely existed. A plant trimmed from top to root, that she was,—a being deprived of the past and of the future. In the first moments of suffering she might have paused and inquired why it had all happened; but as no reply was forthcoming from the blue sky, or from the fields and forests about her, resignation ensued, and wrong remained wrong, while the sunshine floated and the birds chirped about her as before. Her heart contracted and stiffened with its own suffering. As nobody appeared to solve the riddles of her life a fixed idea seized her, and she lost faith in the death of her dear ones,—she thought her husband was walking about some-where carrying on his arms the crying child, both being anxious to return home. Insensi-ble to all other thoughts she was seeking the two everywhere, and traced her way to the club room where she had first seen her hus-band. Unfortunately she did not follow those she was seeking. A strong arm was ready to assist her and to restore her mind to its sane condition. This was energy wasted, yet it helped toward preserving her life. Gustave's affection, surrounding her from all sides with loving care, tied her to the world. His voice made her remain behind, even if it never ech-oed within herself, and she did remain, al-though in a passive state, like a dead thing and not like a human being.

Such was the bodily and mental constitu-tion of the widow. She stepped forward in the room and remained standing a short dis-tance from the door like a statue of stone in its sinister majesty. The atmosphere was sultry and clogged with smoke, and the air even resounded with the strain of a somewhat frivolous and jovial song.   On this impure ground appeared the figure of the widow like a water-lily above the turbid waters.   The company became quiet,—a sign that she was honored; even Augustinowicz appeared tolerable. Some remembered Potkansky, others bowed their heads before her misery, and there were many who did homage to her beauty.   Gustave approached the visitor, took the warm shawl from her shoulders and retired to the corner where Schwarz was seated. The young man watched the scene with intense interest mingled with awe.   Gustave began talking to him.

"There she is," said he, in a half whisper.

"I understand."

"Don't go near her.   The poor one, every new face is a source of disappointment to her, —she always watches for her husband.

"Do you know her long?"

"Two years.   I acted bride-man and witness at the wedding"—a bitter smile. "Since his death I see her every day."

"Wassilkiewicz mentioned you had given her a great deal of assistance."

"Yes and no. Some one had to look out for her interests, and I did so, hence the meagre results I obtained. Do what you please: Work, run about, and lend assistance: Misery remains misery, and it sometimes makes one feel desperate."

"How about the family?"

"Which family?"

"His relatives — —?"

"Hang them!" cried Gustave in excitement.

"Are they not wealthy and influential?"

"They add to her unhappiness. So-called great men,—yes. But hypocrites! But we are not yet at the end of the drama, and they shall regret the wrong they have done to this poor, innocent girl. If a child—even if a child belonging to that family would beg a piece of bread of me to relieve his hunger, I would rather throw that bread before a dog."

"You're too sensitive."

"Schwarz, you wrong me!   True, I am but a poor devil, and should not speak too much aloud, but a short while before Potkansky died in the hospital he regained consciousness and said to me: 'Gustave, I leave my wife to your care; you will guard her when I am gone.'   I replied: 'I shall guard her.'   Then he said: 'You will not allow her to starve.'   I told him no.   Then he said: 'Don't let any one harm or wrong her.   If any one does, revenge it.'   He went out like a consecrated candle, that is the whole story."

"Not all of it, not all of it, brother!"

"Wassilkiewicz told you the rest?   Well, let me say this: I have no one on the wide earth to care for,—no father and no mother,—I am working day by day with nothing in view but" —he motioned toward her—"her alone."

Schwarz, inexperienced as he was, now had occasion to become acquainted with the feelings of a passionate soul, and to watch the rise

of an overpowering force in the life of a young
man like himself. Gustave, who appeared a
dried-up, misanthropic specimen of mankind,
literally teemed with power and life; he
seemed taller and manlier, shook his hair like
a lion's mane, and the blood mounted to his
cheeks.

"Well, gentlemen," began Wassilkiewicz,
"the hour is late, and not all of us are going
home to sleep. Let's have another song before we bid good-night to one another."

The pianist of girlish appearance struck a
few well-known chords, whereupon a few
voices joined, followed by the whole choir, in
the singing of the renowned "*Gaudeamus.*"
Schwarz walked up close to the piano and was
standing a few steps from the window in the
full light of a lamp. In a short while the
glance of the young woman became fixed at
the student's clearly outlined profile. She
seemed to struggle with her thoughts. Suddenly she arose to her feet, pale as marble and

with a feverish fire in her eyes.   She stretched
her arms toward him and cried:

"Kazimir, at length I found you."

Hope, astonishment, joy and awakening
struggled in her voice.   Quiet reigned in the
room.   The eyes of the company sought the
figure of Schwarz, and those who had known
Potkansky experienced a singular sensation.
The tall, powerful frame of the young man
was, as it appeared in the strong light, strangely alike to that of Potkansky.

"I never noticed it," said Gustave to himself, as they returned home.—"Well, it's over,
but she is sick and excited.— —He really has
a close resemblance to him. — — — Upon my
word, that cough of mine is becoming worse
and worse."

CHAPTER II.

Schwarz considered matters carefully before deciding upon a definite line of study.

"I have pledged my word of honor that my life should not be spoiled," said he to Wassil-kiewicz, "at least by no foolish act of my own. That is the reason why I am not anxious to decide."

As a matter of fact, the University was exercising a great power upon him. Young men from different parts of the world came and went, like flocks of young eagles. They flocked around science, drew from the fountain of wisdom, from life; they gave and received, and kept what they received within themselves, or scattered it on life's highways; they stagnated, fell, fought and conquered, some going straight to the bottom and others remaining at the surface of the unruly ocean on which they kept floating. There was movement and stir,—life reigned absolutely. The University appeared both a common refuge and a whirlpool of effervescent youthful intelligence. It opened its doors every year, ready to receive and make use of the many new possibilities and to lead forth the realized ones. It seemed a center of promise and rejuvenescence, every year it poured forth its waves of fresh forces offering light to the blind and abundant sources of nutrition for the enrichment of the human soil. The boat of Joseph Schwarz was, too, floating on the face of these waters,—where was it to land, and which course would it take? The different departments possessed equally great charm and attraction; they all tempted him in one way or another, while he was making his choice. Finally he embarked in good earnest and registered his name at the Department of Medical Sciences.

Whatever happened, he must become rich —this was his main consideration in deciding the question.

The main reason why he had faltered in his resolution was that he was greatly attracted, by virtue of his former state of longing, toward science as a whole. Philosophy and law attracted him greatly, but the natural sciences appeared to him the greatest triumph of the human spirit. This view had been fostered already in the gymnasium, where he received instruction in chemistry from a young professor, an enthusiast who had, in parting, placed his hand on the boy's head, saying:

"One thing is certain, my boy: Outside of the natural sciences everything is mere nonsense."

True, the rector had afterwards assured the boys that theology was the exclusive road of beatitude for the human family, but Schwarz, whom the rector had often designated "a genuine heretic," greeted this assertion with such a grimace that the entire class roared with amusement and a thundering speech of admonition was delivered on his behalf.

So he chose the science of medicine as his

specialty. In some respects Wassilkiewicz was responsible for the choice, as he possessed a powerful influence among all freshmen. Once, during a private assembly, a philologist who was talking rather spitefully than sincerely arrived at the result that whoever devoted himself to science was obliged to renounce life and happiness forever.—"The story runs," said the speaker, "that an Icelandic fisherman became so enhanced by looking at the aurora borealis that he could not withstand the power of the waters. He became seized by the suction of the waves while staring at the strange light, and the sea swallowed him, unable, as he was, to withdraw his sight from the enchantment. The aurora had taken possession of the fisherman's reason."

"Such is the relation between science and life," continued he. "Whoever meets the sight of her wonders and bows down before her may be swallowed by the depths of life, but the spell prevails."

One is sometimes approached by principles

6

that cannot be truly accepted; yet, a large amount of courage is required to enjoin them. For this reason the speech was followed by a general silence, only Wassilkiewicz sniffed, arose and spoke as follows:

"Empty words, and nothing else. A Suabian may court science in such a way, not we. I am certain that science exists for mankind's sake and not mankind for her sake. Let the Germans be reduced to vellum. Your fisherman was a fool; if he had touched the rudder the aurora would not have become invisible, and the man might have returned home with food for his children.—Again something new! Our people suffer from hunger and cold, and you stand prepared to be a burden to the world instead of a helper. Tetwin, Tetwin, think of the meaning of your words and not of their sound. You mistake stupidity for wisdom. To-day you seem ready to sacrifice happiness for a few yellow fragments of paper. Blindness! In your moments of pain and sorrow you will feel a genuine yearning to-

ward love and felicity.—In my home at Samogitia there are sitting two persons of old age
in a poor little cabin. They tell each other
things of me,—of the golden-haired prince of
fairy fame. How could I become worthy of
their thoughts if I buried myself among my
books without a thought of them, and left
them alone in their old age? Why, I should
consider myself a scoundrel, if I did.—Well,
here I am, but science does not obscure them
to my view. Not I alone, but everyone has a
right to enjoy his daily bread,—everyone who
labors in his fields. Honor to science, but the
wise man must not recoil from the duties of
life. A wise man, a learned man, — —
and he is unable to button his own waistcoat,
to educate his children, to care for his wife.
Why not attempt to bring the requirements of
science in closer accord with those of life?
Why not pervade science with life and fertilize
it through life?"

This was the substance of Wassilkiewicz'
speech. It lies beyond our province to decide

who was right and wrong, and we have re-
corded the speech only because Schwarz, who
had a practical turn of mind, was greatly influenced by it. He pondered over it, reflected, considered the views expressed therein,
and the latter had a decisive influence upon
his choice.

People may say what they want, but every
one enters the world endowed with certain dispositions. From his entrance into life
Schwarz was holding more closely to the matter than to the idea. He never was an admirer
of dialectics, and was disposed to view things
as they really were rather than artificially
beautified.—Man's train of thoughts is two-
fold: One is eternally winding its way from
the center; the other seeks the center. One is
eternally revolving about things and facts,
peering into their nature and imparting life
to them, eventually tracing their origin and
development: These are creative talents. The
other seizes the facts as they appear, connects,
disjoins and arranges;—scientific talents. The

former embody a creative power, and the latter are of an investigating nature. They stand in the same relation to each other as a spendthrift to a miser; as inhalation and exhalation. It is difficult to determine the advantage of a creative faculty over that of remodeling or reforming. Both possess active power,—so does the stomach. The perfect equilibrium of the movements from and toward the center implies genius.

Schwarz possessed the latter of these faculties,—that of concentration. He realized it, and this saved him from much unnecessary trouble, giving him ample opportunity to measure cause as well as effect. He never attempted anything that he knew was impossible to himself. In addition to this he was possessed by enough eagerness for the discharge of self-imposed duties. The spirit that liked to view things soberly was equally anxious to treat them in accordance therewith. But in order to view things soberly it was necessary to possess a fair measure of thor-

ough knowledge. He did not fancy guessing,
—he must learn the nature of things. Consequently, the young man acquired nothing by
halves. Like a spider enveloping a fly in its
web, he wove a net of thoughts around his
objects of study, drew it towards himself,
sucked it out and digested it. His mind was
highly elastic. He had great desires,—the
sign of youth, and preferred originality to
second-hand knowledge. Very often he re-
jected commonly accepted views because they
were supposed to be supported by an author-
ity that he refused recognizing.

CHAPTER III.

A month passed. It was a beautiful autumn evening, when the sun lingered on the
church steeples and in the far-away open
plains. In the little garret occupied by
Schwarz and Gustave the light had not yet
disappeared. Both men were eagerly making
use of the last rays of daylight; they sat quietly, intent upon their work and anxious to
make as much use as possible of the fading
day. A short while before Gustave had returned from town; he was pale and sniffed
worse than ever; on his face rested an expression of trouble, restlessness and of ill-con-
cealed, yet secret sorrow. There was a feverish glow in his eyes expressive of intensive
heartache. Both were silent, but evidently
Gustave was anxious to open a conversation.
He turned toward Schwarz more than once,
but seemed unable to utter a single syllable

and turned his attention to the work before him. Finally he jumped to his feet, and asked in a tone of pent-up impatience:

"Is it late?"

"Six o'clock."

"Why don't you go visiting Madame Potkansky, as you are in the habit of doing?"

Schwarz arose and turned toward his friend.

"Gustave, you brought me there according to her wish,—you, yourself.—But it is useless discussing this matter, it would be unpleasant to both of us, and we understand each other perfectly well. Let me tell you that I shall visit Madame Potkansky neither to-night nor to-morrow, nor at any time hereafter. I promise you faithfully; here is my hand."

They faced each other in silence. Schwarz reached out his hand, and Gustave realized the delicate character of the matter;—finally he pressed the hand of his friend. Both found it difficult to express their thoughts: One felt the need of a hearty word, the other was seeking in vain a phrase of thanks, but they remained silent. Mankind is often subject of singular feelings—such feelings as are really the opposite of what one expects as a reward of noble deeds. Schwarz promised Gustave to discontinue his visits at the widow's home. Whether he loved her or not, it was a great sacrifice on his part, as she was the only bright spot in his troubled, monotonous existence. Even if his worship of her meant the expenditure of but a few moments now and then,—moments otherwise devoted to peaceful rest and wrestled with difficulty from the long hours of patient application,—to give up such moments meant depriving rest of its pleasure and called forth a vacant feeling instead of a sense of higher sentiment. Schwarz had renounced the latter, however, without wavering. But as soon as Gustave left the room Joseph's countenance expressed regret, resentment, and even anger. Did he mourn the past, or did he repent of the promise just made?—No.—When he reached out his hand to Gustave, the latter hesitated in taking it. Renouncing the sacrifice of an energetic soul would have meant the same as covering the deed itself with a tint of ridicule, even in the mind of the one by whom the sacrifice had been made; that implied ingratitude and would have helped planting the seed of hatred in the fertile soil of selfishness. To accept the offer of the rival was equal, on the other hand, to place a mind rich in pride open to a critical examination,—was equal to receive an offer prompted by charity and unsought for. And pride generally prefers the position of the creditor to that of the debtor. No wonder, then, that Gustave's lips quivered, as he passed along the streets, and that bitterness and irony filled his thoughts.

"Better and better!—An act of grace.—Remember falling on your knees every day before Schwarz in recognition of his gracious decision! Dear me, what a life."

Thoughts of a decidedly unpleasant character occupied him more and more. He grad-

ually lost sight of himself in his reflections—
the indefinite woe of things and matters in
general. It cost him considerable trouble
even to stop and reflect upon the joys of life
that he had hoped to gain some time.   His
soul and his feelings seemed disconnected. A
picture of internal strife and struggle had
walked along the streets, vainly realizing
where he went, when suddenly a familiar bass
voice sounded close to him.

"Hallo! Hallo! Hallo! Hallo!"

The horseshoe is finished — —

He glanced around and caught sight of
Wassilkiewicz and Augustinowicz.

"Where are you going, Gustave?" asked the
one.

"Well,—I was—where,"—he referred to his
watch. "It is too early visiting Madame Potkansky, so I had better repair to the club."

"You'd better pay your visit anyhow."

"Why?—How so?"

"Woe,—woe!" cried Augustinowicz, lifting

his arms and reciting, without regard to the by-passers, in a loud tone:

"The castle and the happy bridal party have become sombre and silent. The old walls are covered by weeds, and the watchful dog keeps barking before the gate."

"You are excluded from the club," added Wassilkiewicz.

"What has happened?"

"Sorrow and terror are brooding there—" continued Augustinowicz.

"Tell me, what has occurred?"

"A calamity."

"What calamity?"

"A horrible one."

"Speak for him, Wassilkiewicz. Talk plainly."

"The trustees of the University have closed our club. They denounce all who take part in students' assemblages."

"When was it published?"

"Two hours ago."

"Let us go and inquire of the proper authorities."

"I advise you to make no steps in that direction. You would merely expose yourself to imprisonment."

"They tied her white arms with ropes—"

"Augustinowicz, do be quiet.—Why did they not do it in the evening. They might have caught all of us like fish in a net."

"No, they were more interested in closing the clubs than catching us. But if anyone should go there hereafter, they would make an example of him."

"Where are you going?"

"Like the tempest rushing forward to let loose its wrath against — —"

"I asked you to keep quiet."

"So said the valiant Rodrigus — —"

"Exactly," declared Wassilkiewicz, by way of interruption. "We are going over to warn the rest, so good-bye to you, or come along with us, if you care."

"I cannot join you."

"Where, then, are you going?"

"To Madame Potkansky."

"Good-bye."

"*Auf Wiedersehen.*"

Proceeding on his way Gustave rubbed his hands as a mark of sincere gratification, and a smile of satisfaction passed over his troubled face. He was pleased with the closing of the club, as it put an end to his fears of a possible endeavor, on the part of the widow, to seek Schwarz in the club rooms when she learned his decision. His apprehension was well founded. Gustave remembered that in spite of all his praying and reasoning the promise of bringing Schwarz to her residence was the only means of keeping her from seeking the club rooms. Now he had nothing to fear. In a little while he touched the bell-rope at the widow's residence.

The door was opened by a servant girl.

"Is your mistress well?" inquired Gustave.

"She is quite well, only she walks about the

room speaking to herself from morning till
night," returned the girl.

Gustave entered the house. The apartments of the widow consisted of two small
rooms facing a garden. One served as *salon*,
the other was a bedroom that received its
light from a high, gothic window, the upper
part of which was equipped with panes of colored glass in different shapes and shades
united into blue and red rosettes. In one of
the corners was placed a mahogany table with
a black velvet cover, on which were placed
two portraits. The one of these represented
a young man of light appearance and with
beautiful, aristocratic features;—this was Potkansky. The other was a likeness of the
widow, on whose lap a little girl, dressed in
white, was perched. Before the pictures lay a
wreath of goldilocks enveloped in black crape,
and a dried-up twig of myrtle.—In another
corner were two beds and an empty cradle.
The green curtains of the latter appeared to
be moving whenever a breath of light from

the colored panes passed across their folds, and it almost seemed as though a tiny hand might at any time be expected to part them and a little round head come into view.—The room impressed one with a feeling of silent sorrow. The acacia leaves outside the window threw dark shadows over the floor and made the atmosphere throb with faint, shadowy glimmerings. Near the door a small holy-water fount, surmounted by the figure of an angel of baptism, had been placed. The head of the statuette was surrounded by a halo and conveyed to the observer a feeling of joy, purity and peace. Just as sorrowful as the place now was, just as joyful and jubilant had it appeared, however, in former days. What a talking and loving chatter this room had witnessed when Potkansky, tired with the toil of the day, had returned home in the evening, anxious to greet his dear ones! At present this was but a matter of the past, and dreariness had taken the place of quiet comfort. The aspect of the cradle was especially touching. It seemed as though a child might still be there. More than once, indeed, did the widow stretch out her hand, during the weeks immediately following her loss, and ransack the contents of the cradle, in the dead of the night, to satisfy herself that God had had mercy upon her and restored the little one to her care. In one word: These walls had witnessed a great deal: The joy of pure love; afterward tears and misery, and finally, a reserved, persistent grief, bordering on insanity.

The little *salon* bore witness, like all other apartments of that description, of a certain elegance and some emptiness. Here, too, the echoes of former moments of happiness were in evidence;—the room was light, orderly but commonplace, adjoining the servant girl's alcove. This was Potkansky's former study. It was difficult to see how the rent of such apartments as these could be defrayed. Gustave managed the affair, however, and only he knew the ways and means, the nature of which we shall learn in time. Whenever Gustave entered this room he experienced a shudder. At the place where she was living; where everything was full of her presence; where everything that was not hers, existed at least, for her benefit, a heavy feeling would always announce itself, overpowering his heart like a mental burden.   Still, this burden gave him nothing but genuine pleasure, and his breath grew deeper and quicker.   Being under the restraint of a secret sensation of felicity he was almost happy and would have been so perfectly if the borderless field of longing had not extended itself before him.   A great longing affixes its stamp upon the character of a human being as a whole; it pervades the blood with its presence, manifests itself in the manner of speech and in the light of the eye. Such a longing knows of no definite wish and is ignorant of the limits of great and small desires.   It demands everything, even though it cannot realize the nature of the yearning, and renders man or woman outwardly cool in spite of the glowing of the heart. At length the man loves and adores woman, regarding her in the light of an angel and wishes her for his wife.—Such were Gustave's feelings on entering the *salon*. His desires and wishes, his longings and yearnings soared about him like a flock of birds.

And there she was,—pale, with a faint tinge of red, probably due to the reflex of the setting sun on her cheeks. Her soft outlines stood out like a silhouette on the background of the window behind her. She greeted him with an almost imperceptible smile. Her apathetic state of mind had given way to a livelier disposition. The sudden, violent shock received through the appearance of Schwarz had aroused her. In only one respect was her mind still wandering; she did not realize whether Schwarz merely resembled her deceased husband or was identical with him. Thus far her abberation prevailed for some time. In a short while, however, light found its way into the dark of her soul, whereupon she asked Gustave to arrange a second meet-

ing between herself and his young friend. In
spite of himself, Gustave consented. She
looked forward to this meeting with great
anticipation of the return of former moments
of bliss. Without seeking the presence of
Schwarz, himself, she considered his presence
essential to the restoration of her happiness.
And when her wish was realized, the past almost imperceptibly glided into, and took the
place of, the present: Her dreams were ful-
filled. Schwarz, realizing this, promised Gustave to give up his visits, reserving for his
friend the task of communicating this decision to Helen. The effect of this communica-
tion might be easily foreseen: The widow
started and gazed at the young man in great
astonishment.

"Where shall I see him, then?" asked she.

Gustave remained mute.

"I must see him somewhere if not here," declared she. "He is so much like Kazimir.—
Gracious Heaven, I am living only in the re-

semblance of him.   Gustave, do you understand — —?"

Gustave made no answer.   The widow's
blind egotism pained him greatly, and he realized fully the nature of the drama in which he
was doomed to take active part.   The nature
of her request was actually the demolition of
his own happiness.   And again,—she was
the one who asked.   Still, he bit his lips and
made no reply.   He, too, had a right to live.
His whole human nature desperately revolted
against her request, and the latter became
more and more urgent.

"Pan Gustave, you will arrange it so that I
can see him.   I must—I will see him again.
Why do you give me such pain?"

Gustave felt a cold perspiration on his forehead.   Passing his hand over his face, he answered with an effort:

"I am causing you no pain,—but,"—his
voice faltered—"he is refusing to come, and
he will—he will not see you," concluded he
in a hoarse tone.

He would have sacrificed a great deal to avoid this scene. Helen covered her face with both hands and sank back in a chair. Quiet reigned in the room, only the rustling of the leaves against the window panes broke the stillness at small intervals,—and there a human soul strove against itself. To reopen the doors to Schwarz meant assisting him in estranging Helen's thoughts from the one who desired to be the only occupant thereof,—to unfetter the spirit of calamity. But his struggle was brief; he kneeled before her and, touching her hand with his lips, said in a broken voice:

"I shall do all I can.—He shall repeat his visits,—come what may,—I shall tell him to come, only it is impossible to say when.—I bring him here, depend upon it."

In a little while he returned home, saying to himself:

"Yes,—he will return. But I shall not bring him there.—In a month,—perhaps in two,—

then I may view the matter in a different light."

A fit of coughing interrupted further meditation on the subject. For a long time he roamed about the streets in an aimless manner, and when at length he returned home the chimes announced two o'clock.—Schwarz was asleep, he lay in the simple bed breathing quietly and regularly. The lamplight fell across his high forehead and the broad, strong breast. Through a feverish mist Gustave stood quietly mustering the strong figure reposing so freely, a picture of health and vigor. His eyes shone with suppressed envy and hatred. For almost an hour he sat there silently watching the sleeping man. Finally he started,—and regained consciousness. A feeling different to the one hitherto occupying him claimed his attention: He was hungry. Having eaten nothing for two days he turned to his shelf of supplies and pulled forth the remnants of a loaf of hard black bread.

CHAPTER IV.

Fall came. The rooms of the students grew colder and colder. Those who could not afford the expense of warming their abodes drew a bed-cover around their feet and toiled away with caps on their heads. Such studies as were furnished with heated stoves became literally clogged with occupants. The club-rooms were closed, and all attempts of reorganizing the institution being futile, owing to the opposition of Schwarz and Gustave, no regular meeting place was obtainable. The desire of Schwarz, whose influence in academic circles was rapidly growing, was to convince his friends of the fact that club life required the expense of considerable time and was of little benefit. He finally succeeded. In spite of all possible countervotes he defended his views in university circles, especially in the assemblies that took place in the abode of Wassilkiewicz, where guests were frequent and numerous. Wassilkiewicz shared his apartment with Karwowsky, the young pianist of pale appearance, who was quite wealthy and defrayed most of the expense of their common necessities.

The friendship of the two young men was remarkable, and even enviable. The one delicate, beautiful and refined, leading a life of noble dreams, loved by everybody on account of his kindness, gliding through life in comfort and even abundance,—the other a genuine Lithuanian, hideous, pock-marked, with close-cropped hair and a strange fire in his eyes, otherwise lively, zealous, energetic and of solid knowledge. In fact, Wassilkiewicz, who acted as guardian or elder brother of his friend, possessed a mind so enthusiastic that his heart might well be said, as people often express themselves, to lie on his open hand. On one occasion, when Karwowsky became dangerously ill, he attended him day and night in the most self-denying manner and could not suppress his tears when at length his friend was out of danger.—The students called them bride and bridegroom, and an old, blind Ukrainian, who went around begging and upon whom they always bestowed munificent gifts, generally mentioned them in the terms of "the kind young gentlemen." One circumstance tended to unite them more closely than all others. They were in the habit of spending together their summer vacations in the country, and the place generally chosen was Karwowsky castle, where young Karwowsky's sister, a sickly girl of unprepossessing appearance, was living. Her rare qualities had won the admiration of Wassilkiewicz, who loved her,—loved her in his own way, with all his heart, with a great faith in himself, and in the firm conviction that his affection was returned The parents did not realize the character of the young man's feelings, and would not have opposed, in any event, the mutual bond between the two. She was anything but pretty; he was acknowl-

edged a youth of honesty and ability, so their
social disparity became of no great consequence. Besides, the parents would not have
ventured depriving their son of a companion,
the association with whom could result only in
the benefit of the boy.

The Lithuanian was distinguished in other
respects,—in the respect of entertaining a rare
degree of affection for his parents,—the old
people, as he termed them. They lived in a
remote part of Samogitia and were very poor
—poor enough to be obliged depending upon
"the boy" for their support. Old Wassilkiewicz was a game-keeper, whose small hut was
buried deep in the forest, surrounded from all
sides by the rustling trees. The evil spirits
said to inhabit this remote place did no harm
to the two old inhabitants of the hut, where
Wassilkiewicz had first seen the light. As a
boy he had spent much time fishing and catching wild ducks along the sea coast, and in
seeking birds' nests along the edge of the
marshes. His inheritance was a healthy,

ready mind. Nature had been his cradle; birds, trees and sea waves were his early associates. Everything from the fern to the beeches that appeared concealing their tops somewhere in the blue sky, lay before him like an open book, the reading of which he had learned by intuition. The birds taught him their rights; once he noticed how the beavers raised a dam in the stream; he knew how, by following the cries of certain animals, he could discover the secret resorts of bees in hollow trees, and learned such tricks as getting young badgers out of their holes; sometimes he would even bring a young wolf home with him. As he grew older, his father taught him reading and pulled from an old trunk a bag of old copper pennies as a means of laying the foundation of his son's schooling. Hard times began: He must learn,— and he did learn. Stating in detail what he learned and how he worked before guiding his course in the direction of the University would hardly be justified. But as it was, the

parents returned his love a hundred fold. How
great their joy, when he returned home during the vacation, accompanied by Karwowsky.   The latter soon gained the affection of
the gray-haired couple, but their own Jasiek,
whom they always mentioned as "our boy,"
was first in all respects.   Often, when the
young men had roamed about in the forest
and returned home late in the evening, tired
with the exertions of the day, the old man and
his wife had retired for the night and were
talking in a whisper of the lads around whom
their thoughts kept constantly stirring:

"This Karwowsky is a fine young man,"
said he.

"But our boy is still finer," whispered the
woman.

"Of course, yes, of course he is."

They never realized that "our boy" was decidedly ugly-looking, but viewed him through
the prism of parental love and considered him
perfect from every point of view.   It is well
known that the form and color of things de-

pend upon the feelings of the one who views them rather than upon their real appearance.

But to return to Kiew and our friends. No wonder that the apartment of Wassilkiewicz and Karwowsky became a focus of academic life, even more so as it was actually equipped with an excellent heating stove. The so-called higher intelligence of the University congregated there and developed a sort of literary evening parties. Everyone who felt a touch of authorship within him made these assemblies their regular place of publication. During the long winter evenings literary conventions were held at fixed intervals. It is difficult to say how many glowing words fell from the young lips on such occasions. The hosts of the company, seconded especially by Schwarz, Gustave, and prominently by Augustinowicz, led the discussions. Schwarz attempted exercising his creative faculties, but with poor success, as he felt a lack of talent and succeeded but poorly in finding a proper

shape in which to express his thoughts as
well as in uniting the thread of the latter with
that of his imagination. His powers were developed, however, in another direction: He
judged correctly and criticised things and say-
ings in a spirited and witty manner. When
he proceeded in the same way against his
own productions, the company roared with
amusement; his derision shattered all the
play of beginners into fragments. His voice
and gesticulation were flexible enough to render such scenes fittingly dramatic. These talents won the admiration of everyone in general, but such youths as sighed before the
moon and played sentimental tunes on their
heart-strings were imbued with no mean degree of respect.

Wassilkiewicz communicated strongly realistic descriptions of the Lithuanian woods and
seas. Karwowsky "committed" lyrical poems
of dew, tears and sighs, mysteriously inter-
mingled and expressive of soft moods. Logics
were unknown in these poems: The shep-

herd loving the tall, elegant birches that return the affection sincerely enough to wither
and fall to the ground when the shepherd
dies.—Good and bad productions were presented and read; there was much comical, or
ridiculous, matter; on the other hand a great
deal of genuine value was produced even if
real genius must be considered scarce. Augustinowicz surpassed all others. Often he appeared before the company in a state of more
or less complete intoxication, with an ink-
stained, dingy roll of paper, covered with bold-
stroked letters. But when he began reading
everything else was forgotten in the intense
interest of his soul-inspired words. Most of
the young men racked their brains to the utmost and did their best to produce the most
subtile essence of their respective spirits: All
their results were trivial and commonplace
when compared to those of Augustinowicz,
who seized pen and paper and, like a true
"spiritual receptacle," commenced writing—
in the midst of noise and loud talking,—re-

gardless of his surroundings,—until the floor was covered with slips of paper all about him. Then he would gather his leaves in a package, carry them to the meeting place of the friends, and read until the audience was listening spell-bound and with secret envy. His figures were remarkably alive and conspicuous, his dialogue excellent and the train of his thoughts not unlike a variegated, diamond-strewed serpent. When he talked of love everyone felt the beating of a rich and warm heart, and his dramatic scenes abounded in supreme power and mighty, awe-inspiring elements.

His talent was most decided. The beautiful thoughts and words fell like ripe seeds from a mature fruit, and yet they hardly seemed prompted by his individual feelings, —hardly appeared to have any connection with himself. They were beautiful flowers grown in a swamp; they were manifestations of a human nature struggling between moral decadence and lofty views.

8

"Well, Augustinowicz," sometimes said his comrades, "if you are able to free yourself from the devil's grasp, you might produce works of eternal value."

"For that very reason I desire to drown the devil within me. Give me something to drink," said he.

Gustave rarely put in appearance on these occasions. He affected a dislike of Karwowsky because the latter was generally admired. The more difficult his existence, and the more clouds that appeared in the horizon of his love, the more irascible and unsociable was he. Passionate and desperate wishes generally lead to similar aversions. Such an outcrop of general aversion to men and things was just at present alive in his soul. He hated all that possessed what he, himself, wanted; he was hurt, offended, and anxious to revenge the wrong he supposed to have sustained, in some indefinite manner. So he kept away from the meetings of the young men, although they all sympathized with him. He was aware of this, but in spite of it he nurtured a feeling of hatred against them all and circled about his one sense of mad, hopeless love. Sympathy humiliated him and roused his feeling of opposition in the utmost degree. The students knew that Schwarz had promised him to abandon Helen; in an unguarded moment he, himself, had divulged it. The effect was a higher degree of kindness toward Schwarz, which was sincerely resented by Gustave. A dark cloud hovered between the two friends and estranged them from each other.

The widow beseeched him more and more impatiently of permitting her to see Schwarz. Gustave realized with repugnance the development of her spiritual life that could cause him nothing but trouble. She clung more and more firmly to the new figure that appeared before her obstructed vision. Her heart, over-excited through longing and separation as it was, always yearned toward the presence of Schwarz, and the very source of her new happiness, as well as the inauguration of a new period of bliss in her life, was a new phase of sorrow and unhappiness in the existence of Gustave.

"I cannot keep quiet much longer," said he to himself. "Come what may, I shall not introduce him in her home a second time."

What lay behind these reflections may easily be divined. Gustave hoped to stupefy himself by hard work: Weakness was sure to follow, and only in his dreams did he experience the happiness otherwise denied him. Once he saw himself kneeling before Helen and holding her hands,—he felt the pulsation of her blood against his fingers. Then he opened his lips and spoke the secret of his life,—his supreme happiness even pained him,—and he awoke! He awoke to see her daily, to enjoy her presence,—but to realize how far she was from himself. He grew more and more thin and sickly; the feverish glow of his eyes seemed to develop into a final flash of pas-

sionate will-power, and this fever seemed
equally exhausting and exciting.

"I wonder how it will all result," he would
sometimes say to himself.

There was, however, something exalted in
Gustave's gloomy excitement. The man was
no idle dreamer. He remained ready, in other
respects, to accept life as it was, and not as it
should be. In spite of his miserable state of
health he managed to pursue his avocation as
ardently as anybody, and strained his power
in the utmost degree. Returning home from
his visits with the widow he required no common degree of mental and bodily agility to
continue his work where he had left it, but he
conquered himself from day to day. He as-
sembled the ablest of the students around him
and formed what appeared in many respects
an opposition against the circle that convened
about Wassilkiewicz. His friends were exclusively engaged in scientific work. He
united with two others in preparing a gram-
mar of the Lettonian language; in spite of fre-

quent quarrels with his associates, he was at
the head of the little body and yielded to his
work what power he managed to wrench
from his mental suffering.

He visited Helen every day.

CHAPTER V.

The relations between Schwarz and Gustave were apparently most agreeable. The two young men shared the little room before mentioned, and no dissension became evident until one day Gustave, on his return home, found the belongings of Schwarz stowed away in boxes and trunks, while Joseph, himself, was engaged in packing sundry articles. Both remained mute, until everything was ready, whereupon Schwarz turned toward his comrade, saying:

"Farewell, Gustave. It is time that I must seek other quarters."

Gustave accepted the proffered hand without uttering a single word. Their parting was very cool.

On his way up the street, Schwarz suddenly found himself face to face with Wassilkiewicz.

"What is the meaning of this?" said the

latter. "Are you intending a change of residence?"

"You know how matters stand between me and Gustave," returned Schwarz, "and so you are able to judge whether I can stay with him in the future."

"But is it right to leave him, as long as his condition is so critical?" pursued Wassilkiewicz.

"Probably not;—I understand what you mean. Still, you may feel certain that I shall do nothing to excite him. You are aware of what I have done for him already;—surely, he should entertain no ill feeling,—and yet — —"

Wassilkiewicz silently pressed his hand.

Schwarz had selected for his new residence a spacious house several stories high, with large, well-lighted rooms, two of which were reserved for his apartments. Besides the money he had received by inheritance, he had succeeded in finding, shortly after his arrival in Kiew. certain sources of income that shielded him against drawing upon his capital for support. Thus he was able to think seriously of arranging his affairs definitely for the future, and the chosen apartments were actually not lacking in a certain degree of elegance. At first sight one was met by the appearance of 'comfort and even of refinement. The bedstead was equipped with a beautiful cover; the floors bee's-waxed, and in the early evening a fire had been lighted in the little stove,—it burned so brightly and warmed the room so well that the premises seemed cosy enough for anyone. The entire house bore an aspect of high respectability. The first floor was occupied by a general with his wife and two dark-looking, hideous daughters; the second floor had been rented by a French engineer, who had sub-let the two rooms to Schwarz. On the third floor there lived an impoverished count who had once possessed great riches, but was at present limited to the temporary use of four rooms, which he occupied with his only daughter and two Ukrainian servant-girls. The neighbors soon caused Schwarz as much trouble as he wanted: The children of the engineer thrummed on the piano all the day long, pretending to practice all imaginable quadrilles ever performed or intended for performance; the general's family was likewise engaged in musical pursuits and seemingly incessant receptions. There was a trudging and jogging at all times of the day on the first floor, and incessant rushing about on the part of the servants. Only the count remained in quietude and seclusion,—no wonder, as he and his family found themselves sitting on the relics of former splendor, like the Jews on the remnants of Jerusalem, pondering over bygone days. Schwarz gave them but scant attention, only once or twice heavy footsteps on the landing caught his attention and he realized that the old gentleman took a walk accompanied by one of his daughters. Being no admirer of titles and rank, as such, he was not at all curious to form their acquaintance. On a single occasion he was met, however, by an incident that excited his curiosity. He was descending the stairway on purpose to go out when his eye was caught by a figure perfectly modeled bending over the banister above and looking at him;—a beautiful head with blue eyes and dark hair. She shaded her eyes with her hand trying to penetrate the dusk of the passage. Realizing that she was observed she withdrew her head from view, and when Schwarz prepared himself to investigate the apparition more closely the girl disappeared up the steps with swift strides.

"One of the young countesses," thought the young man.

The countess became, however, an object of more than passing interest to Schwarz. Without realizing how or why he often saw, while sitting before the fire at twilight, the dark eyes shaded by the hand; the white forehead surrounded by curly locks of dark hair,— and he imagined hearing the determined stride of her feet on the stairs. Several days hence, when pondering over his work late at night, his ears caught the strain of a melancholy Italian air sung by a woman's voice. The youthful, sonorous tone attracted the attention and interest of Schwarz: sentimental, passionate pleas, vows, pledges and reproaches were interwoven in the song in the most dramatic and captivating manner, and the young man, unable to resist the spell, found himself an eager listener. The voice proceeded:

"E tu spietato, da un'altra amato
 Dici e dilirio, e non è amore
 Piange mi vadi, nè a me tu credi
 Or tu sci barbaro, che non hai cuor,"—

"The countess," thought Schwarz, "is singing."

The next morning he did not understand why a sudden inspiration made him interrupt washing his hands and imitate the pathetic strain:

"Or tu sei, tu sei barbaro!"

But soon the little episode was forgotten, and the widow began occupying his thoughts once more.—"The woman loves me already," thought he, "or she may have bestowed passing interest upon my appearance,—which of these I do not know."—For a brief while it pained him that he had ever seen her: "A singular, strange woman. How dearly she must have loved Potkansky; — — then, there is Gustave;" his eyebrows knitted themselves; "whether I see her or not, the affair will kill Gustave.—Well, everyone must answer for himself. I wonder in what light she regards my absence."

He often found himself recalling the moment when she cried: "Kazimir, at length I have found you!" He realized that to return to her, love her and be adored by her was a matter wholly dependent upon himself. This thought of a possible love deprived him of his night's rest. He realized youth's yearning toward affection and love, and his heart expanded with a feeling threatening to overpower him. Until that hour he had become so deeply impressed with the personality of no

other woman. The blue eyes and dark hair
of the countess sometimes occupied his mind,
but behind it all floated the vague dream of
the widow. He also remembered having
once seized Helen's hand with an urgent desire of kissing the fine white fingers, when he
noticed a dangerous gleam in Gustave's eyes,
and realized the effects of jealousy. Often an
indefinite feeling of regret of his uncalled-for
promise made itself felt, but he always said to
himself: "I pledged my word; I shall not return to her."—Something else was at times
troubling his mind,—something that might
appear to persons of mature age and feelings
in a paradoxical light,—namely, his quiet
mode of living. His scientific studies presented no great difficulties; no point of learning appeared irrational or impossible, and he
did not exhaust his vigor;—it all tended to
produce a sensation of periodical weariness.
Young and healthy men, such as soldiers,
sometimes feel an inclination to become hard-
ened and gain experience through actual

struggling. The desire of battling that seems
so unreasonable in after years is felt during a
certain period of life as an unqualified condition of existence. The soliloquy of Schwarz
in Gustave's room immediately upon his arrival at Kiew was the first premonition of
such desires. He was ready to throw his
glove at something, or someone, in the name
of science, or ideals,—throw it before the feet
even of the world itself.—Young eagles like
to try their wings in the heights, between the
fleeting clouds and the dark abyss. Even the
most trivial of human beings will realize, before reaching the state of the snail, moments
when the wishes of the eagle are not unknown
to him.

Schwarz found himself in this state, but no
one realized his condition and approached him
closely enough to give him any assistance.
He had more or less comrades, or friends, in
university circles, and he enjoyed the prospects of still wider circles; but beyond his own
narrow limit everything was in darkness be-

fore his eyes. Something happened, however, that roused him from his state of dullness. Augustinowicz started a matter strongly in opposition to Joseph's ideal of a student's honor. Hence all the clubs and coteries determined to pass resolutions excluding him from their numbers. It was the first instance in which such a matter was broached, as the students always attempted to keep affairs of this kind within the limits of their corporation, —now the measure was, however, filled to overflow, and prompt action demanded. The nature of the matter is immaterial; enough is to state that the students' court of justice was decidedly in favor of the expulsion. There was no possibility of appealing the decision to any higher tribunal, as the university authorities always affirmed decisions of this kind, and an eventual appeal would merely tend to attract general attention to the affair. At present the excitement of the students was very great, and no one except Schwarz felt the least degree of sympathy with Augustinowicz. Joseph, however, undertook to create a strong opinion in favor of his friend and to save him, if possible, from complete disgrace.

"You intend to expel him?" said he, during one of the tumultuous meetings while the matter was being debated,—"you intend to expel him? Are you blind to the fact that he may bring trouble to us even when you have removed him from the University? What measures do you propose to adopt in such a case?—Then, where will he go, and how do you expect him to support himself? What occupation will he find for himself?—And again: Do you know why he fell before the temptation?—No, you do not know.—Why, ask whether he ever received a substantial dinner!—Let him show you either of his feet, the right or the left. Why, expel him if you find a solid sole on any of his shoes. So far as I am concerned,—the deuce take any one that fails to agree with me,—I hold that it is our duty to save, instead of ruining the man. Give him a helping hand,—give him bread,

9

I undertake to assist him on my own responsibility."

"Who will assist him on his own responsibility?" inquired one of Joseph's antagonists.

"I do," returned Schwarz, in a thundering voice, stamping the floor with his foot.

A general uproar ensued. Wassilkiewicz supported Schwarz with the full extent of his influence; others claimed that expulsion was the only reasonable conclusion of the matter. The debate grew boisterous. At length Schwarz arose, and, turing to Augustinowicz, addressed him personally:

"They will forgive you. Come with me!"

On leaving the hall, Schwarz rubbed his hands and cried gleefully:

"It would have been a great pity to a man of such abilities.—I should like to know if they will prove able to effect the expulsion even in my absence."

"Schwarz, why did you wish to save me?" asked Augustinowicz.

Joseph looked at him severely.

"I pity you," said he, in a slow, measured tone. "I feel you deserve it—to-day."

— — — In the meantime another drama was being played in the apartments of the widow Potkansky. As already mentioned, the main characteristic of her life was that she seemed unable to live unless guided and governed by some all-absorbing feeling. The first time she was successful and developed into an ideal wife and mother. At present she believed that Schwarz had been destined to fill the empty space in her existence; but one month passed after another without bringing her nearer to the realization of her wishes. Her longing grew stronger and stronger, as she became aware of the opposition to her wishes on the part of Gustave. At length a collision between these two powers, directly opposite, as they were, became unavoidable.

"Unless you bring him back to me," said she one evening, during one of their stormy interviews, "I shall, myself, go and seek him. I am ready, Gustave, to kneel before you and ask the favor you promised me. You often said that Kazimir told you to protect me—I beseech you, in his name—oh, God in Heaven, you cannot realize how I suffer. It would all be clear to you if you, yourself, were married, or at least if you loved someone—you never did."

"I—I never did—," whispered Gustave with an expression of deep sorrow in his eyes— "Probably you are right.—Indeed, you can have noticed nothing—seen nothing. I do not know if I ever loved any one except — — except you alone."

He threw himself down before her, and for a moment the room was perfectly quiet. Neither of the two persons moved; the widow leaned back in her chair, covering her face with both hands. Gustave was kneeling at her feet. The pause became oppressive; both were highly agitated, but even a moral pain has its crisis. Gustave rose and soon came to his senses. He roused her and commenced speaking slowly and abruptly:

"Helen, forgive me. I should never have said it, but I have suffered nearly beyond endurance. The first time I saw you is nearly three years ago—in the church. The minister lifted the chalice and you bent your head before its sacred presence; — in those days I might yet be counted among church-goers.— I saw you often since then, and—oh, forgive me—I do not fully realize how it came. Then, you met the man with whom your fate became united,—I said and did nothing. Even to-night I meant to keep still,—I never thought of approaching you; but when you said I had never loved any one — —. In that point you are wrong. It is hard to give up all hopes and one's dearest wishes;—forgive me! Before this day closes Schwarz will be here;—he is noble and good. Give him your love and —remain happy. Good-bye, Helen."

He bent down and kissed the hem of her dress, then arose and, with a parting glance at the figure in the arm-chair, opened the door and was gone.

The widow was alone in the room.

"What did he say?" whispered she.—"What did Gustave say?—That *he* was to return to me. — — Is it a dream? No, no, he will come!"

CHAPTER VI.

Augustinowicz had taken up his abode with
Schwarz in good earnest. What a difference
between his former life and his present way of
living. Hitherto he had never possessed a
snug corner;—Schwarz provided one for him.
He was deprived of bedstead, bedclothes and
like articles of necessity;—Schwarz bought it
all. He possessed no clothing worthy of the
name;—Schwarz furnished him with all he
needed. He was starving, and Joseph shared
his meals with him. Warmed, nourished,
properly dressed, combed, washed and shaved
he assumed the appearance of a new being.
Augustinowicz was, as already mentioned, a
man of weak character, bred by adverse conditions of life and a product of these factors.
Under Joseph's strict surveillance he soon developed in a way hardly to be expected. He
commenced leading a proper, frugal life and

to rejoice in his own radical change. Where
formerly he had evinced no sense of propriety
he now appeared governed by modesty and
shame, and he avoided everything not in accord with his elegant dress and begloved
hands. The most difficult matter lay in persuading him to give up his immoderate use of in-
toxicating liquors, but his opportunity of re-
lapsing into old habits was reduced to a min-
imum, as Schwarz kept him within reach and
never permitted him to engage in any matter
on his own account. Once in a while he allowed him taking a glass of some strengthen-
ing beverage, but otherwise never permitted
him the free use of money. It is difficult to
imagine the air of impatience with which Augustinowicz watched Joseph's preparations for
allowing him to enjoy a glass of wine. He
seemed, on such occasions, to be rendered pre-
maturely delirious; imagined the smell and
taste of the beverage; how he carried the glass
to his mouth; how it touched his organs of
taste, and how it pursued its course down into

his internal regions. At such episodes
Schwarz almost invariably drank to him in
order to deprive the alloting of such necessary
doses of their humiliating character.

In the course of time Schwarz gradually
treated him with more consideration by speaking of university affairs and discussing with
him things in general, finally also by taking
him into his own ways of thinking and doing.
It is unnecessary to state that Augustinowicz
accepted all these marks of recognition as his
just dues; that he repeated Joseph's ideas
on the proper occasions, prefixing such formu-
las as "In my opinion — —," and so forth. In
other respects few would be ready to recognize his old self in his behavior. The same individual who had, a short while ago, professed
unqualified disregard of the common laws of
propriety, would at present attempt to prevent any improper turn of the young men's
conversation by such a remark as: "Gentlemen, do not forget the consideration of our
deportment." The students laughed, but

Schwarz smiled satisfaction at the results of his endeavor. He pursued the same studies and worked jointly; the latter arrangement enabled Schwarz to appreciate the accomplishments of his friend, and to recognize how he seemed to realize no difference between difficult and facile questions. In the case of Augustinowicz, an astonishing degree of intuition seemed to take the place of reflection; a less durable, but comprehensive memory replaced learning by hard work.

Wassilkiewicz was a frequent visitor at the dwelling of Schwarz and Augustinowicz. At first he was accompanied by Karwowsky; afterward he came alone, at a definite hour each day. His discussions with Schwarz on important scientific and other questions were always becoming more confidential. The two men mutually realized the value of their attainments, each anticipating something great and glorious on the part of the other. Their relations, founded upon mutual respect, seemed to assume a character of lasting friendship.

Both occupied a position of leadership among the students; the initiatives of important matters always proceeded from them, and as they invariably agreed there was an uncommon degree of harmony in academic circles—conditions tending towards leading collegial as well as scientific pursuits into the proper channels.

"Tell me," said Schwarz one day, "what is generally thought of my affair with Augustinowicz?"

"Some regard you a veritable demigod," replied Wassilkiewicz, "others are making you object of ridicule. One day I paid a visit with one of your antagonists in the interest of our library movement; I met a great many of his friends,—they happened to be discussing the matter of Augustinowicz and yourself.—Do you know who defended you more eagerly than any one else?"

"Who did?"

"Guess."

"Lolo Karwowsky?"

"Not he."

"Then I cannot imagine—"

"Gustave!"

"Gustave?"

"Exactly. He told those who ridiculed the affair so many agreeable things that I'll warrant they may not forget them for a considerable length of time.—You know his manners. I almost expected they would have torn him to pieces."

"I never counted on him for any such support."

"Is it not because you have not seen him for a long time?—Well, over head and ears in that unfortunate love affair, I suppose.—But he is a man of no mean ability, and I feel quite sorry for him.   You know him as well as any one,—is he ill?"

"Oh, he is never quite well."

"What is his complaint? Asthmatic troubles?"

Schwarz made an expressive movement with his hand.

"Asthma, — overworked himself,— organic troubles of some kind."

"I am sorry for him."

At this moment steps sounded in the passage; the door was opened, and Gustave, himself, entered the room. His appearance was singularly changed. The color of his face seemed transparent and literally bleached. His countenance carried the traits of a corpse; an ashy hue lay over his temples, and the forehead bore the appearance of ivory. The pale lips; the dark hair; the long, unkempt beard, and moustache contrasted strangely to the bloodless skin. He looked like one just recovering from the effects of some severe illness, but carried an air of self-command and determination, coupled with desperate resignation, about him.—Schwarz was astonished, even somewhat puzzled, and hardly knew how to start the conversation. Gustave, however, came to his assistance at once.

"Schwarz," said he, "I am obliged to ask a favor of you. You promised once never to visit Madame Potkansky again.   Take back your word."

Joseph looked at him in a manner indicating serious displeasure. The subject was by no means agreeable to him, so he merely replied:

"I always was accustomed to keep my word."

"Certainly," returned Gustave in a quiet way, but this is an extraordinary case.   In case of my death your promise becomes entirely void,—and I am ill, very ill. She is in need, however, of friendly assistance, and I can do nothing beyond what I already did. I find myself unable to watch over her, and must give it up, as I am in great need of rest. My power is nearly exhausted.—Otherwise, you may as well realize the full extent of the truth; she loves you, and probably you do not, yourself, regard her in the light of total indifference.   In fact, I was in your way;—now I am ready to withdraw myself. This step is the result of circumstances that force me in spite of myself, so there can be no sacrifice on my part. I loved her dearly and even entertained a slight hope that she might return my feelings, —but I was altogether mistaken."—He lowered his voice.—"Nobody ever loved me and my life always was unhappy.—But there is no other course for me. I have suffered for years and years and stored up a great deal of experience, but without avail. All that I now wish is that she may not be left without care and comfort.—If it were possible for me to make a sacrifice I might become her guardian;—Schwarz, do that for me. You possess both energy—and means,—and she loves you, so there is no danger of your being submitted to such trials as I have experienced.—The world has used me badly—well, don't let us speak of it. I never could think of doing anything to harm her; my love is above all such thoughts; but I would not like to submit her to sorrow and suffering by leaving a duty toward her undone.—Sometimes it becomes our duty to accede to the wishes of others. Go,

go,—go to her. We have been living together, and we have shared something, you and I;
—in a certain sense you are obliged to grant
my request, and therefore I repeat before you
that I am sick and weak and do not know
whether I may ever see yourself or her again."

The tears started in the eyes of Wassilkiewicz, who turned toward Schwarz, saying:

"Schwarz, you must promise all that Gustave asks of you."

"I shall go to her," returned Schwarz, "and
I promise you to protect her. Here is my
hand and my word as a man of honesty."

"Thank you—," said Gustave. "Go and
tell her all."

In a little while Gustave and Wassilkiewicz
were alone in the room. The Lithuanian remained quiet for some time, as he needed to
compose his feelings. At length he exclaimed
in a tone of heartfelt sympathy:

"Gustave, poor Gustave, how you must suffer in this moment!"

Gustave made no reply. He breathed

heavily, bit his lips, and a spasm passed over his countenance. Finally a loud sobbing broke from him, and a sensation of complete weakness passed over his body.

———

Three days later Schwarz and Wassilkiewicz were sitting in Gustave's room. Through the beautiful evening air the moonlight floated into the garret, filling the space with a silvery haze. There was a candle burning near the bed of the patient, who had preserved the use of all his senses, as yet. The head resting on the pillow was almost beautiful. His extreme paleness; the tall, white forehead, and the expression of his features. One thin, white hand rested on the cover, the other was pressed against his breast. A faint shimmer of yellowish light fell from the candle over the figure of this man who was literally a martyr of his own feelings.—The opposite corner of the room was almost entirely wrapped in darkness.

Gustave was in the act of detailing to
10

Schwarz his duties to the widow Potkansky. From time to time he addressed a few sentences to each of the two men, but he spoke with difficulty. Wassilkiewicz at length arose and began wiping the moisture from the forehead of the patient.

"I would like to tell you," said Gustave,— "they send her two thousand Polish gulden every year, but she is in need of five or six thousand.—The rest has been brought together by me,—put aside the light and reach me something to drink. — — I worked,—took away from myself—saved and sacrificed my night's rest. Sometimes I did not eat for several days,—lift me up and raise the pillow —I am beginning to feel faint. — —In the box over yonder you will find thirty rubels for her. — — It is growing dark before my eyes — — let me rest—a little — —"

Once more the room became quiet, only a mouse was rattling among some papers in a corner.—Death was approaching.

"I would like to have finished the work in

which I am engaged," continued Gustave. —
— I should like to know whether there is a
heaven and a hell.—I never prayed,—and yet,
—and yet — —."

Wassilkiewicz bent over him and asked
quietly:

"Gustave, do you believe in the immortality of the soul?"

The other nodded assent; he was unable to
speak.

The room was filled with beautiful, soft music. On the silvery rays of the moonlight a
host of angels in white robes and with lumin-
ous wings of white and gold glided into the
room. They hovered about the bed, filling the
narrow space with the humming of their
wings.—Such was the departure of Gustave's
soul.

The burial was conducted with a display of
considerable festivity. All the leaders in university circles were present. From this moment
the public mentioned with wonder and admiration the self-denial and the solid knowledge

of the deceased. Gustave's accounts showed that he had in fact succeeded in earning a yearly income of about four thousand Polish gulden. The entire sum had been expended for the benefit of the widow,—he, himself, had led the life of a dog. Such disinterested and carefully concealed activity secured for him a lasting reputation among the admirers of brave and noble deeds. A number of unpublished scientific treatises indicative of excellent talent and able research were found among his papers,—and a diary. The latter contained simple, almost barbaric accounts of a lowly, unhappy life,—an apology for unreasonable, passionate, blind, youthful devotion,—an account of real as well as imaginary sorrows, pains, struggles, inner suffering and their outward manifestations. The higher life of an over-excited nature revealed itself in its dark solemnity. The effect of looking into this labyrinth could be nothing but startling and awful—feelings that are almost unknown to the everyday, in the words of the

poet, "devilishly gilted world."   The diary
was read before a select assembly in the apartments of Wassilkiewicz, and some even
thought of publishing certain portions of it,
but the idea failed to materialize.   Augustinowicz, however, undertook the preparation of
Gustave's necrology, and produced a vivid
sketch of the life of the deceased friend.   He
pictured his years of happy childhood and his
life henceforth.   The treatment of his life's
spring-time was so attractive that it almost
seemed as though the warmth of summer had
touched the author's own spirit.   Then the
colors grew darker and darker.   Life began to
seize him with its iron grasp, threw him about
and made its tempests howl and roar around
him.—Again the light burned bright and clear
when the one woman whom he loved appeared
before his eyes surrounded by a halo,—and he
reached out his hand toward this bright star.—
"The remainder is well-known," wrote Augustinowicz.   "May he enjoy his last, long sleep
thinking of her.   The sky-lark will sing over

his grave,—will sing the name of her. May
he sleep quietly. The fire is extinguished, the
spell is lifted;—that was Gustave."

As a rule mankind will say a great deal of a
man after his death, while during his lifetime a
great deal of opposition fell to his share. We
shall take leave of Gustave and follow the fate
of Schwarz, our hero. In him nothing had
suffered a material change, only he moved
about, since resuming his visits with Helen,
in a state of absent-mindedness and quietude.
Augustinowicz, however, entered into his new
life with strong determination. In the general's apartments there was as much noise as
ever; the engineer's family thrummed at the
piano with their former perseverance, and the
countess sang as usual during the evening
hours. Gustave's room was let to a shoemak-
er with a wife, two scrofulous children and con-
stitutional poverty. Where great and noble
thoughts had taken form and shape and pon-
derous words had fallen from young and warm
lips now reigned the sound of a cobbler's tools.

Helen was not even made aware of Gustave's death, as Schwarz kept the fact from her, fearing the effects of too great excitement. Some time later he noticed how she received the intelligence with an expression of sorrow, but without despair.

CHAPTER VII.

Obedient to the promise Gustave had received on the fatal day already mentioned, Schwarz had sought an audience with Helen and left her with a feeling of something stronger than mere interest. Returning home in the dead of the night he enjoyed the aspect of the sparkling stars, the beautiful weather and the cool, but highly refreshing breeze that wafted across the Dnieper river. Light flocks of mist arose and formed long bands above the eastern horizon. There was music in the air and music in Joseph's heart. It seemed to him as though the clear night celebrated with himself his possession of life's joys. Bright memories and great hopes constitute true happiness. The pressure of Helen's hand still rested in his own, and he hoped and longed for the moment when she would consent to place her future life in his care.—How won-

derful it all was. In parting she had said to
him: "Think of me." Who would give up his
dreams when the dawning of the next day is
full of bright promise?—He felt that he loved
her. Under the impression of the grand and
solemn nightly scenes surrounding him at all
sides,—the blinking of the stars and the awe
inspired into him by the dark, vast space beyond, he lifted his eyes toward the sky and
whispered:

"If you do exist, you must be all goodness
and good will."

In spite of the doubt expressed by these
words they signified a great deal in his case.
He had begun recognizing goodness and
good will as one of God's essential properties.
At this moment he was really convinced of the
existence of a Creator and Lord. There is no
reason why we should wonder at these words,
or place them in opposition to Joseph's professed realism. The lips that framed them
had touched the cup of beatitude.

When Schwarz returned home Augustino-

wicz was already asleep; his snoring penetrated even as far as the outer passage. It
sounded almost harmoniously, with alternate
long and short breaths, and in varying tones.
Schwarz awakened him. He had determined
to share his joy with a friend who knew him
sufficiently well to recognize his transport.
Augustinowicz, however, stared blankly at
him and began expressing his feelings thus:

"In the name of — —."

Schwarz laughed aloud.

"Good night," said Augustinowicz. "To-
morrow I intend to have you give an account
of yourself,—at present I prefer to sleep. Good
night."

The following day was Sunday. At an early hour Schwarz prepared the tea, while his
friend remained in bed smoking a pipe the
head of which he was closely scrutinizing.—
Both were thinking of the events of the previous day. At length Augustinowicz broke
the silence.

"Schwarz, do you know what I am thinking of just now?"

"No, I do not."

"I tell you, it is not advisable for any one to permit himself being captivated by the first woman he meets. By Jove, it's not worth the trouble. There are things a great deal better than that."

"How did you come to think so?"

"By meditating over this pipe. Mankind often becomes accustomed to one certain mode of thinking,—grows together with it, so to say;—and then all one's great castles in the air materialize not even to the extent of such a puff of smoke as this."

A large cloud of smoke arose from his lips and floated about the ceiling. A lengthy pause ensued, and was again broken by Augustinowicz:

"Schwarz, did you ever fall in love, before you became acquainted with Gustave and Madame Potkansky?"

"Did I ever fall—fall in love?" repeated

Schwarz, fixing his glance at a glass he was holding in his hand. "Fall in love?—Well, I may sometimes have experienced some faint fluttering of the heart, but it never brought me out of my fixed course;— it never disturbed the state of my affairs in any perceptible way. To tell it plainly, I never experienced the state of mind to which you refer."

Augustinowicz raised the long-stemmed pipe above his head and recited in a pompous manner:

"Woman! Emptiness! Fickle being!"

"Why do you say so?" asked Schwarz, with a smile.

"I quote from memory.—Well, in my case it was all so different. A few times I may have experienced such fits as cannot fail to become the fool's share. Once I even made a serious attempt of becoming a better man;— the attempt proved futile."

"How did it all end?"

"Decidedly prosaically.—I was giving lessons in a wealthy man's house. There were

two children, a minor son and a grown-up
daughter. I gave lessons to the boy, and I
loved his sister. One evening the tears started
to my eyes, and I opened my heart before her.
She evinced some embarrassment, afterward
she laughed aloud and ran away. You cannot imagine, Schwarz, what an ugly laughter
it was, and how heartless were her acts, as she
could not help noticing that I was in dead
earnest,—and besides, she, herself, led me into
it. Finally she even complained before her
mother."

"And what measures did her mother
adopt?"

"She told me I was a ragamuffin,—whereat
I made a deep bow. In the second place, our
relations were to terminate at once, and, third-
ly, she threw five rubles before me. I accepted the money, as it really belonged to me,
and employed them to the end of getting
drunk,—I kept on drinking all the night and
the following morning, and—"

"And then?"

"— and then I started anew and continued all the day long."

"Did you continue long in that graceful way?"

"No.   On the fourth day I was seized with a fit of crying, and henceforth, after I had been somewhat cured—of love, I mean, and not of the effects of drinking,—my attempts of falling in love again were numerous, but I declare they all were most successful,—so they were, on my word of honor."

"Are you at present without hopes in that direction?"

Augustinowicz reflected a little, finally he answered:

"I am.   Women are not worthy of worship on my part.   As much faith as I once placed in them,—as sincerely as I once honored and loved them,—as great is my feeling of their unworthiness of becoming the best reward of man's work and toil —But this feeling excludes that of love.   Do you understand what I mean?"

"And happiness?"

"Don't speak of it. As it is, I whistle when growing sad, and envy takes possession of me—."

"Envy! On what account?" interrupted Schwarz, throwing a swift glance at his companion.

"On account of your relation to Helen.— Don't draw together your eyebrows, and don't wonder at my familiarity with your affairs.—Dear me, it is but natural that I should speak from experience. Let me tell you that I might be very likely to fall in love with Madame Potkansky, and would even prefer a woman of her kind to a great many others. But—don't let me give you any trouble on that account."

"Go on."

"I really was afraid that the widow Potkansky might gain my affection. No doubt she is unhappy, but by the prophet's beard, what need I care? All I care to realize is that everybody takes it for granted that whoever dwells near her becomes inspired with a feeling of eternal bliss,—it is handed down from one to another, like gospel truth. — Upon my word,—well, I would not run the risk of becoming the testator of such a bequest,—not even to make one of my friends happy."

Schwarz placed his empty glass* on the table, turned toward Augustinowicz and said coolly:

"Probably so, but inasmuch as I occupy the position of the testator, you will be kind enough to mention the bequest in a way more suitable to its dignity."

"Well, I am treating the matter seriously, and desire to waste no time in pondering over the question who or how Madame Potkansky may be.   All I care to discuss is what you must do.   My attitude is that of an interested spectator;—nay, I am talking even to the disadvantage of myself.   The problem lies right here,"—Augustinowicz sat bolt upright in the bed,—"I know you as well as her, and she

---

* *I. e., tea-glass.—Trans.*

throws herself upon you!—the initiative on the part of the woman,—bah, that won't do!— Love must be conquered. In the course of a month or so you will grow tired of it; you'll wish her at Jericho.—Schwarz, I want you to become happy. Marry Helen as soon as possible."

Schwarz looked even more vexed than before, and replied briefly:

"I shall do whatever I consider most proper."

In fact, the idea of marriage had not yet occurred to him. Having kissed Helen's hands he had bestowed no thoughts upon the possible consequence of this act. He could not help being vexed when some one reminded him of his duties in this direction,—especially so because his own conscience supported the exhortation on the part of the friend. In one day, perhaps in two or three, he would, himself, have realized the same. But the fact that the appeal came from a source not within himself robbed the idea of the charm of being the

11

spontaneous act of love and presented the matter as a question of duty and obligation. Toward evening Augustinowicz met Wassilkiewicz.

"Are you aware that Schwarz is paying his respects to Madame Potkansky?"

"What then?"

"She is furiously in love with him. Think of the fact and reflect upon the duties of Schwarz in this case."

With his usual quickness of mind Wassilkiewicz replied:

"Exactly. To return the feeling."

"And then?"

"Well, they must decide for themselves, I suppose."

Augustinowicz grew impatient.

"Another question: What would you, yourself, do in a case of that kind?"

"If I loved Madame Potkansky?"

"Yes."

"I should marry her without much speculation."

Augustinowicz pondered a while and then replied, in a tone of deep conviction:

"You know that I owe much to Schwarz. So I think he should receive at least some good advice from me. He is placed in a remarkable situation,—there are certain laws of honor that should not be left out of consideration. It would give me great pain to know that any one might ever have a right to tell Schwarz that he had acted in a manner not fitting the common laws of right and justice. I say it openly, but would prefer not telling him directly. You may do so, however, as you have a great deal of influence over him."

Instead of consenting to do this Wassilkiewicz grew angry.

"What right have you to poke your nose into the affairs of others?—Let him consult his own intelligence. At any rate he has not paid her his respects for any great length of time.—And again, what feelings prompt your words and your interference? If Helen is in any way subject of your consideration, I should prefer—; but this is only one instance of your tendency toward meddling in the affairs of others. You are merely seeking an opportunity of placing yourself in an important attitude and make use of imposing phrases. Don't play the part of a fool. Of course you may lose your cozy quarters in case of Joseph's marriage, but this is the least consideration. Really you never know when you are in earnest and when acting in some rôle. On my part, I am not afraid on Joseph's behalf,—I wish to be like him in all respects.—And what does it all matter to yourself? You possess not a grain of discretion."

"Keep your sermons from me.—Then, you refuse to interfere?"

"If the matter goes on without the perfection of some definite arrangement I shall speak to Schwarz,—I may even decide to force him marrying her, but interfering at present I regard in the light of sheer folly."

Augustinowicz left him in a state of humili-

ation, although he realized that the Lithuanian
was right,—and that the steps on his own part
were merely a manifestation of impertinence
and of a desire to place himself in an attitude of
importance.

CHAPTER VIII.

A few months passed. Winter was followed by spring, and spring developed into summer. —The matter had preserved its former character. Schwarz loved Helen, but the days passed without the perfection of any definite arrangement in view of the days to come. Something happened, however, that threw a shadow between them. On a beautiful summer day Helen tied the strings of a bonnet under her chin, threw a light mantilla over her shoulders and placed her hand on Joseph's arm, whereupon they went out intending to enjoy a walk together. The sunshine was quite hot, although the time approached 6 o'clock in the afternoon; there was dust in the air and an expression of warmth on all faces. They passed a number of Joseph's friends, some of whom greeted the couple in a cordial way, while others absolved their duty with a nod and turned back to glance at the young couple. Schwarz had grown taller and manlier, and his countenance indicated a greater degree of self-reliance than before. Madame Potkansky bore the appearance of a young woman at the time of her early engagement. Her blue hat bands fluttered before the wind, and her general appearance was well calculated to attract the attention of the by-passers. She leaned on Joseph's arm in a graceful, unconscious manner and enjoyed the sun and the fresh air so well that nothing appeared able to dispel her new feeling of joy. Schwarz paid a greater amount of attention to her than to their surroundings.—They sometimes exchanged a few words—remarks that always will pass between lovers and are as important to them as nonsensical to all others. Their conversation took a more serious turn, however. Helen asked Schwarz to accompany her to the grave of her late husband.

"In summer," she said, "there is so much shadow in the churchyard, and a long time has passed since my last visit there. You know that I must not forget him, although you will take his place, Joseph. Let me pray for him now and then."

It was immaterial to Schwarz why and for whom Helen prayed, so he replied with a smile:

"Well, my dear Helen, keep the memory of the dead ones in your heart,—but give your love to those who live," he added, bending his head toward her face.

Helen's reply was a slight pressure of Joseph's arm, a glance and girlish blush. Schwarz took a firm hold of the fine, slim hand that rested on his arm—and was perfectly happy. They continued their way along a path leading to the churchyard, and in a short while caught sight of Augustinowicz, who approached them, smoking a cigar, accompanied by two ladies, evidently a mother and her daughter. The latter was led by Augustinowicz, while the former, being evidently oppressed by heat and exercise, followed in the rear. Augustinowicz was evidently in a jovial mood: his companion often amused herself so heartily that she was obliged to stand still and recover from a fit of merriment. In passing Schwarz he blinked at him, indicating that he was at that moment at peace with the world and its entire course. Joseph asked Helen whether she had ever made the acquaintance of Augustinowicz.

"His appearance is familiar to me, but I never learned his name," said she. "When Kazimir died he approached me on some occasion, but since then I never noticed him."

"He is one of the ablest idlers I ever knew," observed Schwarz.—Some one told me he was infatuated with you."

"Why do you tell me that?"

"For no purpose whatever,—but it is really wonderful how everybody seems to be drawn within the circle of your charm."

"That seems the only power the world has permitted me to keep, dear. You cannot imagine the sorrows and troubles inflicted upon

me ever since my days of childhood,—in fact,
you do not know the story of my life.—I was
educated in a most aristocratic family. The
master of the house cared for me and guarded
me as though I were one of his own children.
After his death I was treated so inhumanly
and submitted to so much humiliation that finally I ran away and sought refuge in Kiew.
An old gentleman took interest in me,—a
dear, very old man, who always called me
Helusia and treated me like a daughter. Soon
he died, however, without leaving any provisions for my support,— and a short while afterward I met Kazimir. You may wonder how
I came to visit a students' club. Believe me,
dear, I was ready to die from shame when I
entered the place, but consider that I had
tasted nothing for two days and suffered terribly from cold. I hardly realized what I did
and what would result from it.—Then Kazimir
approached me—but at first I did not like him.
He laughed and was happy, while a faintness
seemed to spread all over me. At length he

asked whether he might find shelter for me. I consented, whereupon he wrapped me in his fur coat and brought me home to his rooms. After I had recovered somewhat from the effects of hunger and cold I realized where I was and cried bitterly at the thought of being alone in such a place. I considered myself wholly in his power, but he seemed to wonder at my tears, afterward he sat down by me and asked me have no fears. I must tell him everything, and he promised to regard me as a sister.—How good he was,—was he not?— From that moment I knew of no want."

There were tears in her eyes, and the beauty of enthusiasm ennobled her whole appearance. Schwarz did not, however, share her feelings. His eyebrows were knitted, and the expression of his features was one of impatience, and even severity. The idea that some casual likeness, some unimportant occurrence might have procured for him the affection of this woman made a decidedly disagreeable impression upon his mind. Potkansky had won her

in a manner entirely different. The comparison gave him pain; he thought of Augustinowicz and proceeded at Helen's side without
uttering a single word. At length they
reached the churchyard, where slabs, monu-
ments and burial places met their eyes on all
sides. The city of the dead was resting peacefully in the shadow of green foliage. A few
persons walked back and forth among the
graves, and here and there a bird was chirping
a mournful but welcome note in the tree-tops.
At certain intervals appeared the figure of
some overseer or attendant.

Helen soon found Potkansky's grave,—a
large burial-place surrounded by an iron fence.
A small mound indicated the resting place of
Helen's husband and child. A number of
flower-vases were scattered about within the
enclosure; at the sides were mignonettes and
different kinds of ornamental plants;—on the
whole the graves were kept in a most desirable, scrupulously neat state, indicating great
care and skilled hands. Schwarz motioned

one of the attendants to open the lock of the enclosure, and while Helen kneeled at the little mound with tears in her eyes and the words of prayer on her lips he addressed the man in the following manner:

"Can you tell me who keeps this grave in order?"

"This lady always visited the place," answered the man, "and sometimes she was accompanied by a gentleman with long hair, but he has not been here of late. He gave orders about the enclosure and paid for all the flowers."

"The gentleman of whom you are speaking is here at present," said Schwarz. "He was buried here about a year ago."

The attendant shook his head as though he might think: "You, too, will rest here."

"Pray," observed he, "pray, sir, what does it matter? Over there, in the city, is enough of trouble and sorrow. In this place one may rest quietly. I often think that God cannot intend to make the soul suffer beyond the grave.

We are suffering more than enough in this world."

Having finished her prayers Helen stepped forward, and Schwarz again offered his arm to her. He said nothing; his heart was heavy, and with or without a definite purpose he took a different road. As they approached the exit he pointed toward a certain mound and said in a tone of remarkable coolness:

"Look here, Helen. This man loved you during his lifetime even more than Potkansky did, and yet you never offer him a single thought."

Twilight was already setting in. Helen glanced at the object that Schwarz pointed out to her and perceived a wooden cross of a dark color carrying the following inscription in white:

"Gustave,—Died — — —, Anno —."

The glare of the setting sun enveloped the grave and everything around it in a reddish haze.

"Let us return home, it is growing dark,"

observed Helen, drawing herself a little closer toward Schwarz.

On their return to the city nightfall was drawing near, but the night gave promise of coolness and pleasant weather. The moon, large and red, arose over the waters of the Dniepe. Steps sounded and resounded in the narrow avenues of the Public Gardens, the sound of piano music penetrated from within one of the pavilions, where a youthful voice sang a *Lied* by Schubert; the strain floated out upon the air of the night and was carried far away,—far out on the steppes, where a post-horn was sounded.—

"What a beautiful night," exclaimed Helen. "Why do you feel sorry, Joseph?"

"Let us take a seat," returned Schwarz. "I am quite tired."

They seated themselves on a bench, and both relapsed into silence, until suddenly a youthful, sonorous voice roused them from their dreams;—the voice said:

"You are right, Charles. A pure woman's

love works the greater happiness when it is
the echo of the voice of a man's soul."

Two young men walked past the bench occupied by Schwarz and Helen.

"Good evening," said both, lifting their
hats.

It was Wassilkiewicz and Karwowsky.—
When taking leave of Helen Schwarz gave her
a long, searching glance, and returned home
at a late hour in a state of great excitement.

CHAPTER IX.

On the following day Schwarz completely regained his equanimity and having enjoyed a long rest he was even wondering at his fears and doubts of the previous evening.

"We all use a great many beautiful phrases," thought he; "but how is reality? Only a fool would renounce happiness. Gustave's fate is a fair proof of the effects of a one-sided, although sincere, and withal manly feeling. Life demands her dues, and I am not fitted to become the hero of a drama. Otherwise I wonder how it may concern any one that I love Helen and she returns the feeling.—Augustinowicz, get out of bed, and be quick about it. I advise you to give an account of your actions and doings yesterday."

"Did you see her face?" inquired Augustinowicz, with a forced sigh.

"Indeed I did.—By Jove, it looked exactly

12

like a radish fresh from the ground,—and the
old lady reminded me of a trough of sour milk.
—Did you really fall in love, old man?"

"Both are tremendously rich."

"Both?—How much does the daughter possess?"

"I would not undertake the calculation of
such a sum,—and she will become yet more
wealthy than she is."

"Wealthier yet,—respecting a husband and
a family, eh?"

"Not in that respect,—but her mother has
arrived here on account of a lawsuit,—and
only think, the defendant is our friend, the
count, who owes her several thousand gulden."

"How did you learn all that?—Do you
know them long?"

"Since yesterday.—Our acquaintance was
quite accidental: She asked me some question
in regard to the streets,—upon my word, I
hardly noticed the question, but no doubt I
dropped some remark about the fine weather

and asked whether they would permit me to
accompany them on a walk.   The old lady
talks a great deal; I learned at once who they
were and why they had arrived here. She asked
me whether I was acquainted with the count,
and I replied to the effect that I was a daily
visitor in his family circle and would be
pleased to use all my influence with him to the
end of bringing about the payment of the
debt. In the course of our conversation I also
called attention to the fact that I am Doctor of
Medicine, of Theology and of sundry other
sciences and arts;—that I had vast numbers
of patients in the City of Kiew. Whereupon
both of them commenced giving detailed accounts of their many different ailments: I
promised to call at their residence and attack
the sickness at its roots."

"Of course you did.—What did the daughter say?"

"She blushed most properly, as one might
expect, but the old lady scolded and made as-
surances by all imaginable saints.   She prom-

ised to extend her special grace and good-will to me until the last day.——So you will realize that I'm quite sure of my game."

"You are extremely candid — —."

"I shall see them to-day."

"The saints?"

"No,—my new acquaintance. I shall advise both to marry."

"And you intend to marry the daughter?"

"Well, you see—I am growing old;—we all are. I hope we may soon be in position to congratulate yourself."

"I asked you already to avoid meddling in the affair between Helen and me."

"Well, but I wish to say that she is wonderfully pretty."

"Oh, don't—" said Schwarz, who was unable to conceal his gratification.

In this moment Wassilkiewicz arrived.

"I was merely walking past the door—," said he. "Charles is waiting for me down below; we both are going to spend our vacation in the country. Schwarz, I wish to have a word with you, and I shall put it briefly.—I had no desire of meddling with your affairs— even in spite of a request on the part of Augustinowicz. But time runs fast. Kindly tell me, what are your intentions regarding Helen Potkansky?"

Schwarz threw the pipe-stem he was just holding in his hand into a corner, sat down and looked Wassilkiewicz straight in the face.

"Question for question," said he. "What is that to you?"

Wassilkiewicz frowned, and his blood was up, but he answered quietly:

"I ask you as one comrade may ask some question of another. Helen does not belong to the class of women that one may love to-day and cease loving to-morrow. Otherwise anyone to whom the memory of Potkansky is sacred has a right to demand a reply to the question."

Schwarz arose and measured the other with a look of intense anger.

"And what if I choose to make no reply

whatever?" cried he.—"Who possesses any
rights over Helen? Who dares to place himself between her and me?"

Now the patience of Wassilkiewicz came to
an end.

"You, a mere siskin,—you probably think
we shall permit you to have your own play
with the poor woman and never inquire about
your intentions! Why, the devil must have
blinded your eyes. You are responsible to us
for the honor of the widow Potkansky, or we
shall be prepared to make you responsible."

They were facing each other for a short
while, as if ready to settle the matter by a
hand-to-hand fight. Finally Schwarz com-
posed himself sufficiently to resume:

"Wassilkiewicz, listen to me. If any other
person had dared approach me in such a way
I should have thrown him down the stairs. I
do not belong to those who permit themselves
to be commanded, and I do not yet comprehend the reason of your interference. It is
hurting my feelings. So I answer you as well

as anyone else who cares to guard Helen's honor that I am responsible to no one but myself, and that I protest against having any action on my part placed in a false light. You and your friends are acting the part of fools in persisting in this unjust and brutal manner. Besides, your words cannot but indicate a doubt respecting Helen, herself.—This is all I have to say. I now leave you and hope you will reach the proper conclusion regarding the way in which you have approached me."—

Wassilkiewicz and Augustinowicz were alone in the room.

"Well," at length said the latter, "he washed your head as thoroughly as you might wish."

"No doubt he did."

"Ah;—do you agree that he really did wash your head?"

"Certainly," agreed Wassilkiewicz.

"Because you did a foolish act.—One must treat him with great care.—He is endowed with a hard skull."

—Schwarz went directly to Helen. He was too excited to find a satisfactory explanation of his friend's actions and realized in a vague manner that the interference of strangers in the matter between Helen and himself could result only in a disturbance of their mutual relations, separating rather than uniting them. On entering Helen's apartments, he found the door of her room closed, and the servant girl could not say what her mistress was doing. He opened the door quietly;—Helen was asleep in an arm chair. The young man remained standing at the door watching her with keen interest. She did not awake; her breath was soft and regular.—At length he approached the chair and pressed his lips against her hand. Helen started and opening her eyes wide smiled like a child that is awakened by a mother's kiss.—Joseph's excitement vanished instantly; he lifted his head, looked straight into her face and said:

"Helen, I think I love you with all my heart, but the folly of some persons hurts my independence and challenges me. I would like to give you new strength and vigor.—Helen, trust me and give me your love."

"I do not understand you, Joseph."

He seized her hand and continued softly:

"But you shall understand me. I am proud to say that neither my love nor my readiness to make you perfectly happy is less than that of Potkansky. But there is a difference in our outward position. He, the son of a magnate, was able to marry you at once and surround you with wealth and luxury;—I am the son of an artisan and must work hard to realize my plans for your happiness and mine. I have no intention of leaving you, but I must not bring you face to face with the cold reality of poverty against which he shielded you. I must not inflict this upon you, as my wife. For that reason I must be sure of your trusting love.—What will you say to me, Helen? — —"

She made no reply, but drew herself toward him and leaned her head upon his breast, as she looked at him with an expression of childish confidence.

"Here is my answer, dear Helen," said Schwarz, bending over her and kissing her lips. "Probably I am thinking too much of myself," continued he. "I have won you neither by struggle nor by suffering,—I have done nothing for you. Potkansky's wealth and Gustave's sufferings—one or the other might always stand between us. Only give me permission to prove deserving of you;—I have both power and energy. I shall not deceive you."

Schwarz thought he spoke quite sincerely, but it is an easy matter to perceive that most of these words were dictated by wounded pride, especially in the light of Helen's position. If he had sought to marry her at once matters would not have changed to any great extent,—at all events not to the worse. In that case they would have shared common apartments, and he would have left Augustinowicz to his fate, giving up all expenses on his behalf. Yet he was conscientiously keeping his promise to Gustave. No change had occurred in Helen's condition of living,—and Schwarz would have married her in the same situation in which she was placed two years previously. What he said of his own ambition was true only in part; the desire of throwing the gauntlet to his adversaries was all evident. The chief motive of his desire of fixing the the marriage at some future time was avoiding a close union between Helen and himself as long as this union was not warranted by genuine mutual benefit.

CHAPTER X.

On his return home Schwarz passed the old
Count and his daughter, who ascended the
stairs. The young lady bestowed upon him a
glance of curiosity and even turned around to
look at him in proceeding upward from the
landing where the young man stopped. Joseph noticed an indefinite smile on her lips and
perceived that she was in possession of great
beauty. He realized a feeling of satisfaction
when hearing her say to her father: "It is the
young physician, papa, who lives on the floor
below." In fact, only a final exertion was
necessary to reach the close of his university
studies,—and he could not hide his satisfaction of being considered Doctor of Medicine.
Joseph's rooms were open, as the janitor was
doing some repairs here and there. From him
and from Augustinowicz, Schwarz succeeded
in gaining some intelligence regarding the

lodgers overhead. The janitor professed no special favorable opinion of any member of the nobleman's family. He grumbled over their covetousness, although evincing a tendency to consider them quite poor, as the house rent was scarcely ever paid when due.—"A haughty young lady," said he, "who is sitting at the piano all day playing and singing. Maybe she is in search of a husband, but what's to be done!"—He tried to dissuade Schwarz from making their acquaintance; "they are proud and haughty, and their pockets are awfully empty."

"Is the Countess long dead?" inquired Schwarz.

"She died about three years ago. The fact is, they were once very wealthy, but the crops reduced them to poverty, sir,—the grain company that used to forward grain to Odessa! He wanted to take advantage of the others, but the trouble fell upon himself. Her ladyship was better than the rest,—a splendid woman. She fretted her life away. They live here already five years."

"Have they any acquaintance?"

"Probably not. I never noticed any."

Throwing himself on the bed to await the arrival of Augustinowicz, Schwarz drank a glass of tea and fell asleep. When he awoke he felt unwell. Although it was growing dark, Augustinowicz had not yet returned. At length he entered the room, however, in seemingly high spirits. The lady whose acquaintance he had made was a Madame Witzberg, and her daughter's name was Caroline. Augustinowicz had given medical advice to both: The young lady must do a great deal of dancing, and her mother required some riding exercise. He had promised to repeat his visit, and Schwarz, too, was cordially invited.

"The old lady told me that a pressure was already brought to bear upon the Count," said Augustinowicz, "but it is really of no consequence to me.—She had called on the old man, but was received by the daughter that lives with him. She said she liked her. The poor girl was terribly frightened when she learned the purpose of the old lady's visit. I put the question to the old 'un why she was so anxious about a few thousand, as she seemed to possess the wealth of a Croesus. She merely replied that her husband's name had been Cleophas instead of Croesus. If it were her own money she would have given the poor people no trouble whatever. It was the property of her child, however. I pressed her hand with much feeling,—I refer to the hand of the child,—and assured on my word of honor that I was all dissolved by emotion. On taking leave I kissed the old lady's hand. The name of the young woman is Malinka,—a beautiful name, although the appellative does not make much difference.—But why are you so pale, Schwarz?"

"I felt ill and cannot fall asleep, though I slept waiting for you. Hand me a glass of tea."

Augustinowicz filled the glass and handed

it to him, whereupon he lighted a pipe and
threw himself on his bed. Schwarz, however,
arose, drew a chair up to his desk and commenced writing. But soon he laid the pen
aside. His thoughts were literally stumbling
over one another: He leaned back in the chair
and allowed them their free course. Many
others would have relapsed into a reverie;
Schwarz compiled and summed up his past
life, considered the present and drew his con-
clusions regarding the future. Arriving at the
latter point he required a great deal of will-
power to reflect soberly. The words, "It was
the young physician, papa," had left a deep
impression. To gain his doctor's degree and
become one of the apostles of science; to gain
power and influence both through his spiritual
and his scocial accomplishments; to possess
wealth and celebrity—to the latter Schwarz
was not at all indifferent;—to attract the eyes
of the multitude;—to call forth a smile and
win the hearts; — —then he was reminded of
Helen. In the matter of his heart's choice he

was free no more. He was fettered, and yet
desirous of attracting the attention of womanhood; of being greeted with a smile from their
lips and hearing them say to one another:
"There is the young physician."—Thus far he
had not realized that Helen might impede his
course, and he determined to pursue this
thought. Their respective age was no objection, as he was twenty-four and she merely
twenty-one. What, then, might be the reason
why he became possessed of the idea that
Helen might sometime become an impedi-
ment in his way? Conscience told him that
the cause was merely his own vanity. He
knew but little of woman's ways, but he would
learn more about them and become master of
them. There were, however, certain other reasons that Schwarz failed to recognize. His
feeling was decidedly weak. Immense depths
of his mind were yet hidden below the surface
that carried Helen's name. He divined the
existence of such depths in an indefinite way,
and the presentiment deprived him of his

13

quietude. At length he scarcely knew whether
Helen might really prove able to counterbal-
ance all his eventual future triumphs.

All these meditations caused Schwarz a
great deal of mental pain. The lamp was burning dimly, and he had almost relapsed into a
slumber when a violent knocking was heard
at the floor below.

"They, too, are awake," said he, and smiled
at the remembrance of the young Countess.—
"How sweet and quiet such a young woman's
sleep must be," said he to himself. "There
is truth in the old saying that a young
girl is like a bird. The man toils along, grows
tired and ponders over matters, while a
woman,—the one up there is a pretty little
bird — — Well it is growing late,—half past
two already, and I am—What is that?"

He jumped up from the chair.

A violent pulling of the door-bell at once
roused him completely. When he opened the
door, with a lamp in one hand and the other
fumbling at the lock, the Countess stood be-

fore him. She was pale as death and was carrying a light the flame of which was constantly in danger of being extinguished by the wind that blew along the passage. Her neck was barely concealed beneath the folds of a night jacket.

"Please help me, sir," said she, in a quivering tone; "my father is dying."

Schwarz at once seized his case of instruments and, motioning Augustinowicz to follow him, hastened after the young lady. He entered a room where a bed that appeared to have been occupied shortly before was standing. The next room was the Count's own bedchamber. He breathed, or there was a loud rattling sound in his throat. Some bloody foam covered his lips, and the face wore a bluish color. Augustinowicz darted into the room, half dressed, the hair hanging disorderly about his head. Both bestowed all their attention upon the patient without heeding the young lady, who was kneeling in a state of partial frenzy at the foot-end of the couch.

When Schwarz and his friend glanced at each other, realizing that nothing was to be done, she said in great agony:

"Oh God, oh God! probably we should call someone else to assist us."

"Go and call Skotnicky," said Schwarz, and Augustinowicz readily obeyed, although he felt certain that the nobleman's life would be extinguished long before he could return to the house with the physician whose name Schwarz had mentioned. In the meantime Schwarz employed all his energies and his presence of mind in the treatment of the patient, bleeded him, and finally, glancing at the clock, declared in a tone of satisfaction that the attack was over and relief would follow.

"Thank God, there is some hope," exclaimed the Countess.

Schwarz repeated that the illness was now under control, whereupon Augustinowicz entered with the famous physician.

Dr. Skotnicky declared that the patient was saved this time, but added without ceremony that a repeated attack would be sure to be attended by a fatal result. He advised to keep the aged sufferer under constant care and not leave him even for a brief moment. Consequently, our friends remained in the sick room during the remainder of the night. Early in the morning the patient regained consciousness and demanded the presence of a priest. Obedient Augustinowicz went out in search of one and returned with a haggard-looking dean or chaplain, who read the commonly used prayers over the nobleman, confessed him, administered to him the Lord's supper and the extreme unction. The count retained his consciousness for many hours afterward, talked with Schwarz, blessed his daughter, spoke of his last will and performed all the duties falling to the share of a dying Christian. The whole day passed before these ceremonies were ended. Toward evening, Schwarz made an attempt of persuading the young lady to seek some rest, as she was almost unable, in spite of her vigorous constitution, to move about the rooms. Agony and loss of sleep had exhausted her power. She attempted to remonstrate, but finally consented before his urgent appeal. Crossing the floor and entering an adjoining room she reached out her hand and thanked him for the interest he took in her father's case. Schwarz now had occasion to study her appearance more closely, which he did. She might have reached the age of twenty, or even less than that, as her figure bore the appearance of early maturity, and was of medium height with a large, but perfect, mouth, blue eyes, dark hair, and uncommonly sympathetic features. The tall, white forehead, was shaded by the hair, and every gesture and movement were in full accord with the genuine type of aristocratic beauty and elegance. The hands were unusually small and delicately moulded.

The patient slept quietly for about an hour after her departure. Schwarz and Augustinowicz had seated themselves beneath the

shaded lamp; both were exhausted. At length
Augustinowicz began talking:

"Tell me," said he, in a quiet tone, "what
will be the fate of the Countess when he"—he
motioned toward the slumbering figure in the
bed and passed one finger over his own neck,
closing his eyes.

"I am thinking of the same question," returned Schwarz.   "Probably the family will
take care of her."

"Suppose no one does."

"We shall be obliged to discuss the matter
with her. They are evidently reduced to poverty; the janitor tells me the payment of the
rent was due long ago.—At any rate, I am
certain there are some relatives somewhere
and probably friends, too."

"Well, we shall be obliged to discuss the
matter before very long," continued Augustinowicz, who was not adapted to remain at
one point for any great length of time.

"Stop," said Schwarz eagerly. "Here is an
idea of my own. Hitherto they have received

no visitors, I think, and the poor young lady cannot remain alone here"—he motioned toward the door of the room where the Countess slept—"after his death.—Say, is your recent acquisition, the Madame Witzberg, of whom you were speaking—is she a lady of pious tendencies?"

"Oh,—like a wafer-box."

"Honest and good-natured?"

"Uncommonly so,—but how may that affect the Countess?"

"I should like to have her take charge of the girl."

"But there is the lawsuit."

"Yes,—for that very reason."

The patient suddenly stirred. Schwarz gave him a swift glance and continued in a whisper:

"The only question is that of the house rent, but it will be settled, somehow or other. Probably there will be a slight inheritance."

"The house rent, yes, the house rent," whispered Augustinowicz. "To prevent fall-

ing asleep, let me tell you a story.—I never
used to pay any house rent; the mere mention
of it would vex me nearly beyond endurance,
and yet I was unable to dissuade any owner
of houses that it was a ridiculous thing.
Finally, however, I succeeded. I was occupying a room in a house belonging to a gov-
ernment official,—a stupid fellow, as dull as
the ears of Midas. One summer evening I was
sitting in a summer house, a cozy little place
in the garden, and had decided, for want of
other occupation, to count the number of
stars in the sky. A dreaming mood came over
me,—you know how a star-lit sky may give
rise to romantic feelings. Then this block-
head was bold enough to walk up to me and
to begin talking all kinds of nonsense; he demanded the immediate payment of the amount
due him.—Well, I arose from my seat, and,
pointing solemnly to the east and the west, I
asked him in a tone of mysteriousness:

"Do you see that vast space and these mil-
lions of heavenly lights?"

"I see it all," returned he in a manner indicating that my tone had frightened him. "But— —"

"Don't speak a single word," said I. Taking off my hat and fixing my glance upon the sky, I thundered out:

"Miserable worm of the dust. Compare to it all your paltry five rubles — —"

He was interrupted by a groaning from the bed. The color of the patient's face turned blue, and his fingers were twisted into knots. Undoubtedly the second attack was in progress. Schwarz rushed up to him and managed, by the use of force, to straighten out his arms.

"Be quick and bleed him," said he, in a quiet but distinct tone.

The room was singularly quiet. In some unknown way the supply of oil in the lamp was just then exhausted. From time to time Schwarz dropped a quick order or made some quiet remark.

"The pulse?"

"Water."

"He is choking," whispered Augustinowicz. Both held their breath, as the lancet was passed into one of the large veins of the arm. —But no blood came. — —

"It is all over," said Schwarz, panting from exhaustion. "Nothing more can be done."

Large drops of perspiration rolled down over his forehead.

"He has lived his time," observed Augustinowicz, to whom the affair was one of absolute indifference. "We did our duty; now let us go down and enjoy the rest we need."

CHAPTER XI.

The Count died and was buried according to Christian rites. A few days after these happenings, Schwarz obtained an audience with Madam Witzberg. He desired to discuss with her the question of providing in some way for the young Countess, as none of her family had taken any steps in this direction, and her father had left but a scant supply of means. Even if a large fortune had fallen to her share, the young lady would have been unable to assume control of her own affairs. Owing to the intense religious feeling of Madame Witzberg, Schwarz very soon succeeded in arranging the affair in a satisfactory manner. He told her at once that the lawsuit begun at her instigation had killed the Count, consequently it was her duty to give some assistance and kind attention to the daughter of the man who became the prey of her avidity. The lady was terribly frightened at the idea of being committed to the tortures of hell, and besides realized that the education of the Countess might be very valuable to her own Malinka. Madame Witzberg was a respectable lady, who lacked, however, the quickness of spirit and the necessary knowledge of the tortuous ways of the world. As a testimony of her experience we may state that she viewed Augustinowicz a pattern of elegance and polished manners; Schwarz, on his part, gave her some trouble by hinting at the real state of the case. It had given her great pleasure, she said, to open her doors to a young man of such distinction. Malinka, who was in many respects like her mother, had taken a fancy to Augustinowicz, and was very anxious to remain in Kiew. Her mother shared this wish and had already decided to make arrangements in this direction: It became a matter of necessity that Malinka should learn the ways of the world and witness life in a large city. Malinka was nineteen and had visited Kiew only once before.   At Zytomir she had been twice, otherwise her life had been spent at home.   Questions of ways and means gave her no trouble; she was well endowed with property.   Her father had occupied the position of a prominent custom-house official, and in spite of this the following words had been spoken at his grave: "Rest peacefully, Cleophas Witzberg.   For many centuries will the population of whole Europe preserve the memory of thy integrity and virtue;"—in spite of these words Cleophas Witzberg left nine hundred thousand Polish gulden to his dejected, sorrowful wife, and he might have hoarded up even a still greater sum if the all-powerful goddess of Fate had not determined upon cutting his life-thread asunder. So he passed away to the realm of shadows complaining of the decision that forced him to abandon such a remunerative occupation. His money was, however, left in the hands of persons who used it with thoughtful care. They assisted poor widows and servants, paid

the wages of their maids and other assistants
with great regularity, paid tithes and absolved
other Christian duties involving both their
bodies and their souls. The young Countess
was received with open arms and was treated
as cordially as though she had been one of
their closest relatives. Malinka was verily
transported with the young, aristocratic lady
that captivated everyone at first sight. She
resolved to treat her with the greatest kindness and offer her all possible assistance, and
raved over the ideal friendship that she expected to spring up between them. On the
whole, Schwarz had succeeded in finding a
most desirable place of refuge for the orphan,
who could hardly have expected better days
in her old home.

The young Countess was, in fact, a person
of most sympathetic appearance. The quiet
and deep sorrow that weighed upon her mind
at present carried the whole person so far
beyond the limits of reality that she could not
be thankful to those who received and treated

her in the kind manner already mentioned. She thanked Schwarz with many tears and reached out her hand, which he kissed. "Upon my word," said Augustinowicz, "I was nearly reduced to mere vapor at her looking at me. The deuce take her; she is a hundred thousand times as pretty as myself."

The new figure, attractive as it was, soon became a part of the existence of our hero. It is but natural that such a woman should make a deep impression upon him. If Future might endow her with angel's wings, or if her beautiful form were inhabited by the hypocritical and dried-up soul of a common mortal, time would show. If life were like an open book and if we were able to inspire human beings with souls, like developing an idea,— if they remained the same as they were before and yet turned out to be different,—in that case things would be entirely different.—A young man or woman may sigh at the idea of having satisfied their thirst with poisoned water. The soul is a fountain that may carry poisoned waters far about the land, and no one may be able to stop the effects of the waters' course. The soul is like a blank leaf; God writes on the one side and Satan on the other, but in this respect God and Satan are merely symbols; the hand that writes is really that of the world. The world writes; good and bad among mankind write, and so do the moments of supreme happiness as well as the times of pain and sorrow. But there are some souls that possess the faculty of the pearl-oyster,— that of converting pain into happiness, like the oyster forms its pearl of a grain of gray, common sand. Sorrows and loneliness assist in evolving this faculty, but not always. Sorrows and loneliness often are the conceal of boredom, emptiness and stupidity. These lovely sisters are never loath to reside at the palaces erected by sorrow and loneliness, and to seek there the things that were never beyond their reach. Loneliness may become fascinating, but sorrow never is, at least to those who are afflicted by it. Loneliness is to the soul what

14

sleep is to the body,—and even more: Quietude dissolves, melts away, eliminates and even almost removes every patch of mist and smoke that may envelop the soul; words and thoughts echo everywhere within the limits of the land of silence,—the soul is limited to a oneness and loses its idea of center as well as of circumference.—All this is named in one word—rest. Loneliness is one of the most unattractive words in the vocabulary of mankind. Loneliness never is lonely; quietude always brings change and variation. What a pity that the misty train of this lady's dress is often carried by a page of too handsome appearance—laziness! Certain poets even maintain that loneliness may be creative; the soul contracts within itself and becomes receptive to a vision from without. For that reason loneliness generally develops fools or wise men, somnambulists or poets.—The young Countess was a great friend of loneliness.

Then, she became a — —?

We shall see. Reality again forces itself

upon us, and the Countess enters into this reality as,—as what? As a young lady;—as one of the world's most attractive objects under the sun;—as a splendid intermixture of blood, flesh, fragrance, sunshine and what else!—And our own illusions! Fly out, golden butterfly!

CHAPTER XII.

The past life of the Countess had been full of sorrow and trouble. During her father's lifetime she was sitting one day after another in the lonely, poorly furnished rooms, listening to the chirping of the sparrows outside the window, or the bragging of the servants in the kitchen. The Count grew tired in the evening and became wearied with the constant emptying of one depleted can into another, as he named the lawsuits that constantly weighed upon his mind. He succeeded in nothing. In former days he was known as a man of ability and power, who desired to figure as an example of the manner in which the aristocracy should prove its interest in commercial and industrial matters; but the outcome of these attempts was the total loss of his fortune. All that he gained was a fund of experience that he would willingly have ex-

changed for a few thousand gulden,—and a
treasure that could not be wasted, namely his
memory and his family pride. Experience
and pride were united, in his case, into a feeling of bitterness toward life, mankind and the
world at large. This was but natural. His
family took no interest in his affairs, and the
few that cared for him did so in a manner
strongly similar to that known from the fable
of the agonized lion and the horse.—If he had
only been blessed with a son!—A young eagle
would have expanded his wings and plunged
into life and light;—but there was only a
daughter. The Count was not blind to the
poor prospects of the girl whose fate was destined to be that of an old maid, or to be married to anyone that might appear on the scene
when he, himself, was no more. For that reason the old nobleman could not bestow upon
his daughter as much loving care as might
have been the case under different circumstances. Still, or in spite thereof, he was very
fond of her, and the girl returned his affection

so much more as his hair was white and he was unhappy; she knew, besides, that he could extend his feeling to no one else. To her he appeared the last volume of a tale, the continuation of which was developed by her own imagination. Sometimes her father would unfold before her, in his earnest manner, the accounts of brave and glorious deeds;—the history of her forefathers, of noble men and ladies fair. Through these tales her mind was revelling in the greatness of the past. Often she thought that someone approached her from the golden background of the legend,— a man of soldierly appearance, with a sword in his hand;—the son of the steppes, ready for the fight. — — Nothing but a maiden's usual dreams! The wide plains sounded and resounded with the praise of his bravery; but he, the fearless, bent his proud head before the lady of his choice.—The usual dreams of a magnate's daughter! She, herself, was to be the chosen lady, and he must necessarily be a Herbert or a Korecky.

—Lula had become aware, however, that Schwarz was a wise, noble and beautiful man, but there is no reason why we should be warranted to state which one of these qualities was the most important to her. The interest she felt in him was evolved in the oft-repeated question: "Might he not love me?"—Instead of attempting any definite reply she would seat herself before a mirror and meet the glance of her own sparkling eyes.—"And if he did love me," said she; "if he were to kneel before me here—and now—"

Such was Lula's thoughts of the man the acquaintance of whom she had scarcely yet made. As the days passed a singular change came over her, sometimes she was even seized with fright and pondered over matters the real nature of which she could not clearly define. She would often move about in a state of apparent indolence and dullness, then she might press her head to Malinka's bosom and kiss her without apparent reason.

As the days and months passed she had

abundant opportunity to see Sohwarz about her. By degrees a change was taking place in the mind of the young man. The lovely child that he had admired was changing before his eyes into a beautiful woman. He was unable to regard her with his former feeling of peace and tranquillity. Formerly he might have placed her on his knee and rocked her to sleep as one may fondle the little ones to make them conform to our wishes; at present he was far from entertaining such thoughts. The idyl was growing in power over both of them, until after the lapse of a number of months, the following conversation took place in the Witzberg residence:

———

"And if you should love some one, Malinka?"

"I should be very happy, my dear Lula, and would love with all my heart. You see, Lula, that if it pleased God he might have given all his thoughts even to me."

"But suppose he could not return my affection?"

Malinka pondered a while and then replied:

"I do not know; I cannot realize what would occur in that case, but it seems to me that there is a difference in such matters, too. —I would be so happy,—oh, I cannot tell, I cannot say how delighted and glad I would be—."

Malinka threw her arms around the girl at her side, clasped her tenderly and overwhelmed her with caresses.

"Dear Lula, then he would have loved me with all his heart."

They nestled close to each other, and each was occupied with her own thoughts. Quiet reigned in the room until at length Lula resumed in a tone struggling between weeping and exultation:

"Malinka."

"My darling Lula."

"Malinka, I love some one."

"I know it. Lula."

"Old man—!" said Augustinowicz to Schwarz.

"What is the news?"

"The deuce take me if I know any news.— Old man, I noticed that you kissed the veil of the Countess. Well, you are a great friend of such procedure,—wait, I am in possession of an old unbrella that you might probably like to submit to the same treatment, and if it fails to suit you, there is my aged overcoat. The lining is torn about the armpits, otherwise it is well preserved. Bring it to me; — — hand me my pipe.—Well, my dear fellow, I know what it all signifies; the old lady is too dull to notice anything."

Schwarz buried his face in his hands. Augustinowicz watched him for some time, scraped with his feet under the table, cleared his throat and at length exclaimed in a tone of genuine emotion:

"Old man — —!"

Schwarz did not reply. Augustinowicz shook him by the arm as a mark of sympathy.

"Well, my dear friend. It's useless to feel sorry or reproach one's self,—at least, you ought to say that you are sorry for Helen."

Schwarz started.

"Helen, yes, you are sorry for her. Your honesty is beyond dispute; but what is to be done?—By jove, go and marry—!"

Schwarz arose. Determination spoke from his broad forehead, and although the knitted eyebrows bore witness of pain and struggle it was evident that his better self had won the battle. He pressed the hand of his friend.

"I am going."

"Where?"

"To Helen."

"To Helen?" repeated Augustinowicz, with a stare.

"Certainly," returned Schwarz. "There has been enough of uncertainty and deceit.—I am going to ask Helen to marry me at once."

He left the house without another word. Augustinowicz opened his eyes wide, shook his head and soliloquized:

"There you see how other persons less fool
ish than yourself act in such matters.

Whereupon he filled his pipe, threw him
self on the bed and puffed with renewed en
ergy.

CHAPTER XIII.

Helen was not at home. Schwarz waited for several hours, crossing and recrossing the room in a state of great impatience. He had firmly resolved upon giving up the false position in which he had involved himself through his interest in both of the young women, the care of whom had fallen to his share. This determination caused him great trouble,—a severe, almost physical pain. Although he had come to ask Helen to marry him, it seemed to him as though all his interest in her had vanished. His heart was drawn toward both Helen and Lula, and while thinking of the one his mind craved bestowing some attention upon the other. He loved Lula in the desperate manner of an energetical, outwardly cool nature, and prepared himself for the meeting with Helen that would no doubt be a painful one. There is nothing more abominable than professing your love of a woman who is really nothing to you; to a manly character such an act implies a degree of hypocrisy almost beyond the limits of possibility. Indeed, Schwarz had loved Helen, but the feeling disappeared even before he was able to realize how deeply his mind was occupied by Lula. When this became clear to him, for one brief moment he wavered. The new turn of his feelings frightened him, and he dared not reflect upon the possible results of the change that had taken place within himself. He attempted quenching the language of his heart; he closed his ears and became watchful of every step he took, fearing the eventual future results thereof. At war with himself, as he was, he anticipated the coming crisis. When Augustinowicz happened to mention, in a cynical way, the affair, in its trivial aspect, Schwarz was forced to take action at once. All prospects of flight were futile; Schwarz took up the fight and went— to Helen. But the struggle had left its marks upon him. There was a fever in his blood, and he could not command the train of his thoughts. Many different reminiscences of words and memories of the past came into view and he believed more than ever that Lula returned his affection.—"Am I right in crushing her happiness?" said he to himself. This idea, singular and desperate, as it was, followed like the parting shot from an enemy and put an end to all his determination regarding the duty that bound him to Helen. Between himself and the Countess there was —nothing whatever.

Other difficulties beset the road that he had outlined for himself. His purpose was honest, but to bring it into effect he was forced to affect a feeling false in every point of view, and to pass the remainder of his days amidst lie and deceit.

"Debased through good acts," said Schwarz to himself. "Why, the very idea may drive anyone mad.—Indeed, life is growing into a complicated affair, and everybody runs after

happiness like a dog may chase for his tail —
—." The young man, being unfamilar with the
dialectics of unhappiness, hardly knew what to
say or to do. In other respects, such a philosophy is not altogether unattractive; a great
many human beings love their own troubles
as ardently as their good fortune.

It began to grow dark, and Helen was not
to be seen. Schwarz thought she might have
gone to the churchyard, and the idea pained
him, he knew not how or why. Having
lighted a candle he resumed his walk up and
down the floor—and suddenly caught sight of
Potkansky's picture. He had never seen the
man and professed no interest in him, this
feeling of aversion being explained, to some
extent, by his dislike of things aristocratic.—
As his glance was met by the lively, beautiful
face in the carved frame, he felt something
akin to hatred.

"At all events her interest in me is only the
outcome of my likeness to him," thought he.

Schwarz was mistaken. His character was

entirely different from that of Potkansky, and
Helen was already interested in Schwarz on
his own account. But the idea of merely occupying the vacant seat of another was ex-
ceedingly distasteful to the young man, who
would have given a great deal to change the
past so far as the relations between Helen and
Potkansky were concerned.

He took a seat and remained buried in
thoughts, until Helen at length arrived. She
was dressed in black, and her gown was especially well fitted to bring the delicate paleness of her skin into prominence. At the
sight of Schwarz she smiled in a timid manner, but there was such an expression of joy
in her smile that the young man could not
help being strangely touched,—his visits had
been quite rare, of late. Happily she possessed enough tact and delicacy to avoid any
reproach that might be alive within her; her
joy was great, as she had no idea of his purpose. Her hand rested in his and the pressure of her fingers was more eloquent than
15

her tongue had ever been. The smile and the outstretched hand were fascinating enough to make anyone love her at first sight. With a sparkling star at her forehead she would have presented herself as a perfect model of an angelic figure. But Schwarz perceived no aureole about her head;—he was blind even to that wrought by Love.—He touched her hand with his lips.

"Take a seat, Helen, and listen to what I am here to tell you," said he. "For a long time I have not been here, and it is time that our former frankness and confidence should return."

She laid aside her bonnet and shawl, smoothed her hair and sat down on a chair. There was a trace of anxiety and even alarm in the glance that she directed toward him.

"I am listening, Joseph."

"Four years have passed since Gustave, on his deathbed, entrusted you to my care. I have discharged the duty as best I could, but our relations have developed themselves in a manner that is hardly quite proper. It must all be different, Helen,—"

He drew a deep breath. The words that must be spoken were his own doom. During the momentary quiet the beating of Helen's heart was almost plainly audible. She grew pale, her eyelids quivered, and she felt the worst was coming.

"It must all be different — —?" repeated she, in a whisper.

"Marry me."

"Joseph!"

She folded her hands like in prayer and stared at him without seemingly realizing the full meaning of the words.

"Be my wife. The time of which I was once speaking has come."

She arose, threw her arms about him, and leaned her head against his breast.

"Joseph, you are in earnest?—Yes, yes, I shall yet be happy. Oh, I love you so much."

She nestled in his arms, lifted her beaming face to his and continued:

"I was sorry and lonely,—so lonely, but my faith in you was never shaken. The heart believes when it loves. You belong to me alone. I am living only through you,—I care for no one else in the world. I am glad or sorry only through you. If anyone should part us I would tear down my hair and tie myself to your feet. I was like a flame that may vanish by the slightest breath of air. Now I belong to you,—only allow me to weep over my happiness.—Joseph, do you love me with all your heart?"

"I love you."

"I have cried so much and so often, but those tears were different from these I am now shedding.—I am so glad, so happy!—Oh, my beloved Joseph! I hardly realize it all."

It was no easy matter to Schwarz hearing her talk in this way. The lack of truth and harmony in which he was doomed to pass his future life was a fearful background of a picture so entrancing, so sweet,—the picture of the woman with whom he was to be united, and whom he did not love.

He arose to take leave.

When he had left the room Helen pressed her hot forehead against the cool window-pane and remained in this position for a long while. At length she opened the window and leaning her head in her hand gazed out into the starlight summer night. One large tear after another rolled down over her face; the golden hair floated over her shoulders, and there was a silvery haze about her figure.

CHAPTER XIV.

A few days hence Augustinowicz was sitting in Joseph's room busily engaged with his final preparation for the approaching examination. In order to heighten the effect of his important task he had lowered the blinds and drawn his table back into the middle of the room. He was standing there with his sleeves turned up, engaged in some important experiment. The table was strewn with glass tubes of different shapes and sizes, bottles with a variety of powders, and in the middle there was an alcohol lamp, the bluish flame of which surrounded the bulb of a retort that quivered with the bubbling of the boiling fluid.—Augustinowicz was a workman of no mean ability; no one excelled him in promptness and accuracy. With a smile upon his face did he follow the progress of his experiment, sometimes humming a fragment of some song and sometimes stopping to deliver himself of an aphorism regarding the trans-mutations of the world. Once in a while he would drop his work altogether, lift his eyes toward the sky and recite in a melodramatic tone:

"Oh, Eurydice, your glance, your voice
Would fill my life with boundless joys.
The Delphian Oracle has spoken
And given me a sacred token;—
Oh, happy me!"—

Or he would sing, in a shaking tone:

"Oh piano, piano!—Zitto! pia—a—ano!"—
or improvise such apostrophies as:

"Fill your pipe, sit down and puff,
Only choose the genuine stuff!"

"By Mahomet," said he to himself, "if Schwarz only were here the work would be much more easy.—He will marry Helen. Well, I should have no objection to such a wife,—in fact, I always took a great deal of interest in beauty and innocence. — — Beloved Helen, permit me — — well, what next? —Oh, let him proceed!"

Someone sounded the bell with great energy, and turning toward the door Augustinowicz intonated:

"Oh, wanderer, come, be my guest!
Step in, sit down, enjoy a rest!"

The door was opened, and an elegant-looking young man entered the room. Augustinowicz had never before seen him. The most prominent characteristics of the "wanderer" were a velvet coat and light pantaloons; besides, he bore the appearance of being well kept and curried; his face was entirely smooth. The expression of his countenance was not decidedly stupid, yet by no means highly intelligent, and he was neither handsome nor commonplace, looked neither benevolent nor irascible; his stature was neither tall nor low, and his nose, mouth, chin and forehead presented no characteristics worthy of special notice.—

"Does Herr Schwarz live here?"

"Certainly."

"Can I see him?"

"It is hardly possible at present, in the dead of the night."

The guest appeared to begin losing his patience, but the countenance of Augustinowicz expressed neither mirth nor malice.

"The owner of this house," continued the young man, "directed me to Herr Schwarz, who is familiar with the residence and conditions of the Countess Leokadia N.—Will you be kind enough to give me such information as you possess?"

"Oh yes.—She is very pretty—"

"Well, this is not the reason why—"

"My dear sir, I am obliged to contradict you. If I had answered: Hideous as night,—would you have been equally anxious to obtain the desired information?—You would not. By the Prophet, you would not."

"My name is Pelsky; I am her cousin—"

"Well, I am not, and never was, her cousin."

The guest frowned.

"Probably you fail to understand me, and probably you are joking,—"

"By no means, although Madame Witzberg always maintains that I am.—Ah, you are not acquainted with Madame Witzberg!—A magnificent lady. I may be permitted to state that she has a daughter, although there is nothing remarkable in this, as a fact. But she is as wealthy as Jupiter, himself."

"Sir!"

"I hear steps in the passage. Schwarz is coming,—or probably he isn't he. I'll bet it is he— — — well?"

The door was opened, and Schwarz appeared. His strong, intelligent features had ripened into an expression of measured energy and will-power necessary to the realization of perfect manhood.

"Pan Pelsky—Doctor Schwarz, on my word of honor," said Augustinowicz, by way of introduction.

Schwarz scrutinized the appearance of the stranger, who began at once explaining the purpose of his arrival, and although Schwarz could not suppress a frown at the information

of the relation between Lula and the young
man, he gave him the desired information
without hesitating. At length he arose, and
bowing the stranger out, remarked that the
Countess would no doubt be delighted with
the fact that one of her cousins manifested interest on her behalf. The matter would have
been still more pleasant, added he, if some one
of the relatives had appeared some time ago.

Pelsky stammered some indistinct phrases
and was evidently much impressed with the
appearance and behavior of Schwarz.

—"Why did you give him Lula's address?"
asked Augustinowicz, when the friends were
alone.

"Because a refusal would have placed me
in a ridiculous position."

"I would never have given it to him."

"What did you tell him?"

"A thousand things, only not the address,
as I did not know whether you liked it or not."

"In any event, he would have been sure to
find her."

"What a surprise at Witzbergs'!   Will you go and see them to-day?"

"No."

"And to-morrow?"

"No."

"When?"

"Never."

"Old man, running away before a danger makes no hero."

"I am no errant knight, no Don Quixote,— and I would rather avoid the danger and conquer than call it out and be conquered.   I am not governed by the spirit of olden times, but permit myself to be guided by my own feelings of right and justice."

A pause ensued.

"Did you see Helen yesterday?" inquired Augustinowicz.

"I did."

"When will you be married?"

"As soon as I have received my doctor's degree."

"Probably this termination of the affair is the best for you."

"How so?"

"Probably I shall make you angry, but this Lula,—by Jove, I can't trust her."

There was a strange light in Joseph's eyes. He put his hand on the shoulder of his friend.

"Don't say anything bad of her."

Schwarz desired that the likeness of Lula, as it was preserved in his heart, should remain immaculate.

"What am I to say," pursued Augustino-wicz after a short pause, "if she makes inquiries about you?"

"Then tell her the plain truth,—that I married someone else."

"I'll tell you, old man, I have decided to give her another piece of information."

"Why so?" inquired Schwarz, meeting his glance.

"Well,—you see — —"

"Speak plainly."

"She is desperately in love with you."

Schwarz blushed deeply: Lula's affection had long been an open secret to him, but hearing this of a stranger's mouth was extremely painful to him. A feeling of relief, mingled with desperation, penetrated him.

"Who told you?" he asked.

"Malinka,—she tells me everything."

"Go and say to Lula that I marry another woman,—that I do so because I love her and consider it an act of duty."

"Amen," concluded Augustinowicz.

When Augustinowicz called at Madame Witzberg's residence the door was opened by Malinka.

"Oh, it is you," said she, with a blush.

Augustinowicz seized her hand and kissed it fervently.

"Oh, Pan Adam," cried the girl; "that must not be, that is not right."

"It must be, it is right," declared he, in a tone of great conviction. "But tell me,"— and he began drawing off his gloves, having already removed his overcoat,—"tell me if you have not received the call of a young man some time during the afternoon."

"He was here,—he will return some time to-night."

"So much the better."

They entered the salon, which bore the appearance of having been prepared for the reception of some prominent visitor. A double lamp was burning on the table, and the piano was open.

"Why did Pan Joseph not join you?"

"I am expecting the same question from the Countess,—at least I expect her to put the question; at any rate permit me to await that event before making any reply."

The Countess soon made her appearance, dressed in black and carrying a few pearls in her hair.

"And Pan Joseph?" asked she at once.

"He will not put in appearance."

"Why not?"

"Busy.—Engaged in planning his future life."

The Countess was seriously disappointed.

"And you assist him in this endeavor?"

"Heaven deliver me from any such task," answered the young man.

"Then it is a difficult task?"

"Like all other undertakings of that kind."

"Really, I am quite anxious to learn more about it."

"Duty goes before everything else."

"I suppose Herr Schwarz is building everything upon this foundation."

"On this occasion it will be more difficult than ever.—But some one is coming;—your cousin, no doubt. A perfect gentleman in every respect."

Pan Pelsky entered the salon, followed by Madame Witzberg. After the usual introductions had taken place conversation turned toward matters of general importance. Augustinowicz spoke little, but reclined in the spacious arm-chair which he occupied and listened to the company's effusions with half-closed eyes and an air of complete indifference.

It was his habit to close his eyes in meditating, and in such moments nothing escaped his attention. The Count had seated himself near Lula and twisted the string of his monocle nervously between his fingers while conducting a lively exchange of opinions with his cousin.

"Until my arrival in Kiew," said he, "I assure you I had not learned of the loss to our family, and especially to yourself, through the death of your father."

"Were you acquainted with my father?" inquired Lula.

"I was not, cousin. You are aware of the many unhappy struggles and law-suits that separated our families. While a boy and during my absence from home I had no occasion to become familiar with the details of these affairs, but my present journey is an attempt of reëstablishing the former relations between our families."

"In what manner were you related to my father?"

16

"Being educated in a foreign country I was never informed of the details in the matter. Of your presence in Kiew I learned quite accidentally, although I was, of course, aware that your father and yourself had long been living here."

"May I ask how you chanced to find me?"

"I am entirely at your service. After the death of my father I assumed control of both our family affairs and the administration of our estate. While rummaging among our family documents and the accumulated correspondence of several generations I discovered that your family arms are not only similar to those of the Pelsky family, but identical with them."

"Then, in a certain sense our acquaintance is due to a mere chance."

"To a happy chance, cousin."

Lula dropped her eyes and fumbled about her apron; after a moment's silence she resumed:

"Really, the matter is of no great consequence to me."

A faint smile spread over the countenance of Augustinowicz.

"I had a great deal of trouble in finding the location of your residence," pursued Pelsky. "This gentleman,"—he motioned toward Augustinowicz—"manifested a singular method in detailing the necessary information. At length Herr Schwarz, one of his comrades, arrived and gave me the required advice."

"My former home was at the same house occupied by the two gentlemen."

"And you cultivated their acquaintance?"

"When my father took sick, Schwarz took care of him and stayed at his bedside until the end came. Afterward he introduced me into Madame Witzberg's house,—I owe him much gratitude."

The smile on Augustinowicz's countenance faded out, and his eyelids were raised in an almost imperceptible degree.

"Is he a physician?" inquired Pelsky.

"He is on the point of taking his final degree."

Pelsky appeared to ponder over something.

"Somewhere abroad, probably at Heidelberg, I formed the acquaintance of a Professor Schwarz, a gentleman of wide literary attainments.—I wonder if they may belong to the same family."

The Countess blushed deeply.

"Oh, I really do not know."

Augustinowicz by this time opened his eyes wide and he turned to the Countess with an indescribable air.

"No doubt," said he, "the Countess is aware of some facts regarding the family connections of Schwarz."

Lula now became thoroughly confused.

"I do not think—I remember—," stammered she.

"You have really forgotten?—Well, I think it is worth knowing that Schwarz hails from Zwinogrod, where his father occupied the position of a blacksmith."

Pelsky bestowed a look of sympathy upon his cousin and addressed the following remark to her:

"I am sorry to learn, cousin, that fatal circumstances have forced you to associate with persons of—of another sphere."

Lula sighed,—but alas! for no good reason. She knew perfectly well that the sphere to which the nobleman had referred would bring her all the help she needed, guard her against the inclemency of the world, and prove more true and sincere to her than this cousin, whose sympathy she did not crave. The fact of her being loath to tell him so vexed and threw a gloom over her.—In the meantime, Madame Witzberg, however, invited the party to partake of a cup of tea. Lula for a moment hastened to her room, and seating herself on the bed, buried her face in both hands. Her thoughts returned to Joseph's room;—"there he is sitting," thought she, "eagerly pursuing his work, and here they mention him before me as a stranger,—a mere stranger. Why was it necessary to say that he was the son of a blacksmith?"

She thought that Schwarz had suffered a great wrong, but still there was in her mind an undercurrent of regret, and even anger. Why should the man of her choice be the son of a blacksmith?

At the supper-table she sat next to her cousin, and listened to his polished conversation in an absent manner. Augustinowicz, instead of pitying her, distressed her with his mischievous remarks, and the spirit of the little company was decidedly nervous.

"Are you not well, Lula?" asked Madame Witzberg, stroking the girl's hot forehead.

Malinka, who was engaged in serving out the tea, turned to the Countess with a smile, asking:

"May I help you to a cup of tea? We are using the Schwarz brand, so you ought to like it."

Lula glanced at the charming figure of Malinka who was seated beneath a large chandelier, in the fulll glare of its reddish light, but in spite of the pointed remark she managed to preserve her composure.

"I shall take a cup, dear."

When supper was over Lula seated herself at the piano that shielded her with the exception of her tall forehead and the regular, finely curved eyebrows. She played one of Chopin's melancholy etudes, and her face preserved its former expression of fear and unrest. Augustinowicz, with his perfect knowledge of music, divined at once Lula's state of mind, but said to himself:

"She is frightened, therefore she is playing, and she plays because her cousin is here."

Returning home, he offered more thoughts to the matter than might be expected in view of his thoughtless character.

"The deuce knows what will become of them and how it will all end," said he.

Reflecting upon the matter he entered his room and found Schwarz poring over large piles of books and manuscript notes.

"Were you at Madame Witzberg's?"

"I was."

Joseph's countenance indicated impatience and curiosity, and he was evidently thinking of submitting Augustinowicz to a cross-examination regarding the doings of the evening. The question that Augustinowicz expected was not framed, however, as Schwarz resumed his work.

A pause ensued.

Suddenly Schwarz brushed aside his books and arose. Having crossed and recrossed the floor a few times, he resumed:

"You were at Madame Witzberg's, then?"

"Certainly."

"Well?"

"Well,—what do you mean?"

"Oh, nothing in special."

Whereupon he took his seat and returned to his books.

CHAPTER XV.

A couple of weeks passed without any change in the conditions of Schwarz and his friends. Joseph did not continue his former visits at the Witzberg home, but Count Pelsky was a daily visitor, in spite of Augustinowicz, who bored him with great persistence, until the Count had become thoroughly loath of him:

"What does the Countess think of her cousin?" asked Schwarz one day.

"My dear friend," replied Augustinowicz, "he is of no significance whatever."

"Which are your objections to him?"

"None, with the exception of his own stupidity. He converses the young lady to the best of his ability, carries a fashionable suit of clothes, wears bran new kid gloves, ties his neckerchief in a symmetrical bow, praises virtue and reprehends vice, says that it is better

to be wise than foolish,—and yet. oh, my dear
Schwarz, he is of no significance."

"You seem to condemn the world by wholesale."

"Again a new hypothesis!   By wholesale,
indeed!—Don't you know that a man's chest
is measured with a tailor's measure, and not
by the standard of Phidias. In due course one
is obliged to laugh, and yet one's heart does
not break;—it is not worth while."

"It is all Greek to me."

"How, then, can I tell you?—Well, an aver-
age man, a man of middle road,—a man who
has committed no dishonorable deed whatever, such a fellow is he.—Better change the
subject and discuss philosophical systems, or
maybe you would care to sing the old *contre-
danse;* what do you prefer?"

"Pray, do let us talk of him," returned
Schwarz with emphasis.

"Very well, reach me my pipe."

Schwarz filled his pipe, lighted a cigar for

himself and commenced walking up and down
the room.

"I gave you no account of that evening, because I had no desire of vexing you," said Augustinowicz. "To meet a desire on your part
I shall, however, be ready to serve you. The
affair has developed in this manner: Pelsky
learned that the old gentleman had left a
daughter behind him; curiosity prompted his
steps in the direction of discovering her where-
abouts. You know that every one is vain in
some respect or other; every one loves effect,
and there is no lack of effect in assuming the
rôle of a wealthy cousin before a poor girl, who
cannot free herself of her aristocratic ideas;—
this rôle is eminently pleasing to Pelsky. Who
would not like posing in such an attitude?
You are wealthy, and you lend the poor girl
a helping hand; you guard her; you astonish
her with polished and delicate words and manners; you ascend to the position of the prince,
—the ideal man—; I say, old man, this is all

pleasing to your own feeling of vanity. Why, it's romantic:

"The steed is snorting; he stamps the ground,—there is the point. A steed, a noble figure;—tears and smiles on her part.—Fate parts them.—They meet again;—agreement in thoughts and views, and—Pompilius will succeed Numa!"

The last words were uttered in a tone of genuine malice.

"Are you talking of Lula and Pelsky?" asked Schwarz.

"Of course. Pelsky sought her for no other reason than that of curiosity, and she is a maiden of rare beauty,—you know she is;— well, the rôle pleased him. Pelsky is a trivial specimen of mankind, an aristocrat, in other words a fellow of no consequence, but—provided he is not especially anxious about a dowry— —!"

"Oh, provided he is not—" interrupted Schwarz, with a sneer.

"Why do you commit yourself to disappointments? You should not at all mind it, being neither a child nor a woman. You knew what you were doing in regard to Helen."

Schwarz making no reply, Augustinowicz continued:

"I say, Pelsky is young and wealthy; she is making a great impression upon him. In that case he may not consider the question of a dowry. The main thing is that she pleases him."

"Suppose he leaves the dowry out of consideration,—what then?"

"In that case Lula will become the Countess Pelsky."

"You think she will consent?" asked Schwarz, with flashing eyes.

"Old man, listen to me. To-day she might possibly refuse, but six months or a year hence things will present themselves in a different light. If you were to interfere, you might conquer him, otherwise—I repeat the statement—otherwise she will consent."

"Why do you think so?"

"Why do I think so? The very first evening I met Pelsky there I heard him make inquiries about you. To what family did you belong?—'I really do not remember,' replied she. I replied to the question by stating that you were the son of a blacksmith;— and there she stood, with a blush on her face and ready to burst into tears for anger.—Now you know why."

Schwarz, himself, was ready to burst into tears for anger.

"You see," continued Augustinowicz, who seemed to grow more interested in the matter than ever, "Pelsky is acting without experience and free will, but he is doing things correctly. Through him she will come into permanent possession of the old title, the glorious reminiscences of the past, the gracious and great connections.—Let me assure you that she belongs, body and soul, to the aristocracy. Do you remember how eagerly we have discussed this question, and how you exerted yourself to make her give up those ideas?—My dear friend, you may be sure that Pelsky is right in flattering her vanity and rousing her egoism; the result will be that she is estranged from us, old man. We are exactly such counts as—well, the deuce, I can't find any proper comparison."

Finding no comparison he commenced sending forth dense clouds and rings of smoke. Schwarz stared vacantly at the floor, until at length he exclaimed:

"Did you tell her that I am to marry Helen?"

"No."

"Why did you not tell her?"

"I said you were engaged in work of great importance to yourself and found no time for visiting.—I wish she will conscientiously and carefully choose between Pelsky and yourself. Your marriage is a matter entirely apart from that problem, but will tend, of course, to decide the affair in favor of the Count."

Schwarz arose and laid his hand on the friend's shoulder.

"Listen," said he. "Suppose Pelsky is the loser and the struggle is decided in favor of myself?"

"The deuce take you, don't press my arm so hard. I may ask the same question of you: Suppose you win the battle?"

Their eyes met, and the hearts of both men shrank with a feeling of enmity. At length Schwarz withdrew his hand, buried his face in both hands and threw himself on the bed. Augustinowicz glanced at him in a disdainful manner, but little by little the angry trait of his countenance disappeared, and when he bent over the prostrate figure in the bed his voice was soft and full of kindness and compassion.

"Old fellow."

Schwarz remained immovable.

"Don't be angry with me, Joseph.—If you conquer him her likeness will be preserved in

your heart,—like a sacred treasure.   And in
that case I shall take upon me to say these
words to her: Angel of light, stay upon the
path of honor and duty that Schwarz followed."

CHAPTER XVI.

Helen was hardly able to realize her own happiness. She had long been making preparations for the wedding. Her cloudy past had disappeared; the night of her existence had been succeeded by a fresh, beautiful daybreak. A woman who, like a shooting star, cannot determine beforehand where and how it is destined to land,—a homeless woman who possessed no hopes of Future,—such a woman was now destined to change her course of life, to make herself deserving of the love of a noble and worthy man and become his wife before God and man.—A quiet life; a life bathed in sunshine was to begin for her, and all her future days were to be passed amidst esteem, love and duty. She understood, or rather felt, the difference between her present prospects and her past days. "Such an existence as mine rarely terminates so happily," said she to Schwarz; "probably I am not at all worthy thereof."—In spite of this he did not hesitate to place the engagement ring upon her finger.—"I am not worthy of so much happiness."

This woman of almost insane tendencies controlled through love, was right. No ideal happiness could develop on the basis of her former life, unless the latter had ceased to flow in its old course. There are certain stars which roam through the infinite space of the universe until caught by the magnetic power of some powerful planet and forced to follow the course of the latter. A similar force had entered Helen's life: The stronger will attracted the weaker one; Helen's course had approached that of Schwarz and became unified with it. The fact that Schwarz fully appreciated her peculiar situation was a source of comfort to her.—"If he desires me to be perfectly happy and satisfied," said she to herself, "I shall indeed be so." Her faith in the power of Schwarz as well as in his sincerity was boundless. Thus the last shadow of doubt and fear had left her,—the fear, unspeakable and undefined, that she felt whenever thinking of her future existence, before Joseph's declaration was made and every grain of distrust vanished.

Dreaming of a bright future, and with a song on her lips she prepared herself for the wedding, and enjoyed like a child the consideration of every fragment of her gown. In spite of her widowhood she determined to dress herself in white. Schwarz gave his assent. As her spirit became strengthened health returned, and she grew active, able and took interest even in the slightest details of the household. Her appearance grew nobler and more beautiful under the influence of bright hopes and views. From a misanthropic being; from a bird whose wings were clipped she developed into a woman, even though the entire basis of her life was the love of her future husband.

The time set for the wedding was drawing near.

———

The moment was approaching when Schwarz would receive his doctor's degree. In consequence thereof he devoted so much time to study that his health began to suffer. Sleepless nights and severe mental exertions bleached his cheeks, he looked haggard and the eyes were surrounded by blue rings. An incessant anxiety of perfecting his work was alive within him and exhausted his strength, but was also tending to make him desirous of doing his utmost to absolve his work as honorably as could be, in order that he might prove able to gain an independent position and make himself felt. Ambition as well as the approaching marriage were powerful spurs in pursuing the end in view. His funds were nearly exhausted. Augustinowicz had already become a burden to him on account of the increase in household expenses necessary to the support of both men. Augustinowicz had abandoned drinking and was by this time earning considerably more than Schwarz. Through music lessons that were generally quite remunerative, he commanded the use of a fair income, but never thought of saving any part thereof for future use, in spite of the fact that the completion of his studies might some day require all his time and attention. As before, he paid his daily visits at the Witzberg home, when Malinka was always ready to open the door to him, feigning to withdraw her hand, which he covered with kisses. The girl was deeply infatuated with him, but it is difficult to tell his own feelings regarding her, as every symbolical thought had left him during the past. His fire had long been extinguished. If his abilities had been interwoven with great desires or passions he might have promised as well as realized a great deal, but his light was like that of the moon, which illumines without imparting any heat. This, however, did not prevent his being a good comrade, a lively companion and a good fellow

all around. If any one might pride himself
of possessing his sincere affection it was
Schwarz. Certain sympathies and antipathies
were not foreign to him, thus he sympathized
with Malinka, but viewed Lula with decided
distrust. The reasons why Lula failed to
please him were not clear. He, himself, gave
a number of reasons. Thus, she was in the
habit of treating him with aristocratic coolness, and besides, she belonged to the nobility.
As a rule he won the favor of women, but this
was due to his irresistible humor and even to
the air of insolence that made him appear at
home everywhere. He possessed the ability
of placing himself on level with any class of
persons that he met. Although frank and
straightforward he was ready, on a moment's
notice, to demonstrate the finest and most polished manners. Whenever the matter was
mentioned to him he would reply that his
power of accommodation was inheritable and
owing to the presence of "blue blood" in his
family. The fact was that he had never

known his parents and had not even learned their identity, but whenever circumstances required he considered himself the descendant from some distinguished family. One of his favorite jokes was that Laetitia, the grandmother of Napoleon the Third, appeared on his family record, and that he was consequently one of the Bonaparte tribe.

In spite of all these accomplishments he was generally more or less completely ignored by Lula. Her interest dwelled upon Schwarz rather than upon his elastic, light-hearted friend. At length she confessed to herself that Schwarz, with his manly, foursquare character, was the real object of her love, and consequently Augustinowicz was entirely disregarded. This turn of affairs caused him a great deal of vexation.—Such was the condition of affairs when Pelsky appeared on the scene. Henceforth, and especially since the visits of Schwarz had ceased, a great change came over Lula. Augustinowicz, being prejudiced against her, viewed her through the

prism of his antipathy, and thought that her
treatment of him would be still more indicative of indifference and even of dislike. Lula,
however, fearing his sharp tongue, changed
her attitude toward him completely. "Heaven be praised," thought Augustinowicz, "that
the human family is endowed with a facile
tongue. I believe she is attempting to prevent strife between Pelsky and myself."   On
different occasions, indeed, words had passed
between them that could not but produce a
most disagreeable feeling in Lula.   In the beginning she made numerous inquiries about
Schwarz, but obtaining invariably the same
reply, she finally ceased questioning.   It
seemed as though she had even thought seriously of gaining the favor of Augustinowicz;
at any rate, her demeanor indicated a certain
degree of softness and secret sorrow.   Whenever he entered the room her eyes sought his
and addresssed to him a mute appeal indicating that she expected news of some kind.—
Her anxiety was quite natural.   Whether

manifestly any great interest in Schwarz, or not, she was unable to conceal her astonishment of being evidently forgotten by the one who had always approached her in a most sympathetic manner. The information she received failed to impress her with a feeling of safety, and it seemed impossible to her that Schwarz could not find time enough, during a period of two months, to call and inquire about her health,—and besides, she had received numerous proofs of his affection for her. The simultaneous arrival of Pelsky and the disappearance of Schwarz began to look significant. In fact, she often found herself pondering over the question whether this double occurrence might not be connected in some way or other. Augustinowicz was the only one who knew anything, but he maintained inviolable silence.

Lula was passing one week after another in a state of trouble, sorrow and excitement. Pelsky was constantly nourishing her illusions by hinting at a beautiful life with wealth and comfort, servants and carriages,—while her thoughts were circling about Joseph's study, and she never ceased to ask herself the reason why he did not come. Pelsky's attitude more and more grew into that of a suitor, and Lula, on her part, being almost desperate with vexation and humiliation, was more than once thinking of marrying the Count, as a testimony of her anger and spite. Family traditions spoke in favor of the nobleman, and it was no longer difficult to see what side would gain the victory. Pelsky exerted himself to dispel all clouds on Lula's forehead, and his efforts were generally successful. From time to time Lula had a remarkable attack of hilarity; on such occasions she would be fairly sparkling with wit, even though a certain feverish excitement was plainly distinguishable. A strong tendency of flirtation was also prominent in her behavior toward her surroundings; her words pleased and stung, attracted and repulsed every one near her. As a rule Pelsky was the sole object of these reckless

oscillations of her temper, and generally he
would drop the mask of a benefactor and assume a slave's demeanor. The more he was
humiliated, the more giddy was she, and whenever he turned impatient and thoughtful, the
greater became her gaiety.

"Malinka," said Augustinowicz on more
than one occasion, "I advise you not to imitate
her manners,—she is a flirt."

"I do not think so," returned Malinka, who
was unable to conceal her anxiety. "Sometime I may call your attention to this matter
and prove you are wrong."

Augustinowicz might, indeed, have reached
a different conclusion if he had chanced to
observe the coquettish Lula after she had returned to her room and burst into one violent
paroxysm of weeping after another. Then,
consolation was entirely out of the question.
The poor girl had no opportunity whatever of
taking any one into her secret. Nobody
knew what struggles took place within herself; during the moments of weakness she was

altogether alone. It is difficult to say how many tears were shed over the supposed perfidy on the part of Schwarz. In former days she had embraced Malinka, her faithful companion, and told her of all the troubles that weighed upon her mind, but at present she did not trust Malinka as much as before, and the girl manifested serious displeasure on account of Lula's passing flirtation with Augustinowicz. Besides, Malinka was not pleased with her attitude toward Pelsky.

Time passed, and Lula began doubting if she had ever cared much for Schwarz. Pelsky was approaching her with wealth and comfort,—and time fled and fled,—time which is, according to the poet's words, "a poor keeper of blooming roses."

CHAPTER XVII.

Malinka made numerous attempts of learning from Augustinowicz the true cause of Joseph's continued absence.

"Why should he tie her hands?" asked she, referring to Lula.

Augustinowicz vowed that Schwarz had no intention of tying the girl's hands; of the real cause he made no mention whatever and always preferred, when pressed for the truth, telling her a lie. He presumed, on the whole, that Lula had already guessed the facts.

"I have told her everything," said he.

"But she keeps nothing secret from me," remonstrated Malinka.

"Schwarz?"

"Well—?"

"Does anything trouble you?"

Schwarz bit his lips but asked no questions.

He hesitated, feeling that any questions he might ask would at once open all the old wounds. Time brought him no relief, and there were moments when he had a strong inclination toward setting aside all considerations of Helen, of duty and of his own conscience. He would sometimes have sacrificed even his honor and self-respect to be free to lean his head against the shoulder of the Countess. The memory of her would not leave him. Hitherto he had managed controlling himself, yet realizing that a short time ago his feelings had been entirely different from what they were now. Formerly his character had possessed a quietude that concealed every abyss within him; at present it was all struggle and storm. From passionate words he did often pass to a melancholy, passive sentimentality, whereat he remembered having ridiculed every expression of that feeling in others, nay, even despised all manifestations of that sort. Such a state of mind was highly adapted to render him inconsiderate of his self-

respect. Augustinowicz was aware thereof.—
Once, probably a month after Joseph's resolve
of abandoning all thoughts of Lula, Augustinowicz awoke late in the night and observed
that Schwarz was yet seated at his desk, intent
upon reading a book. In the bright glare of
his student's lamp Joseph's light beard and
pale countenance stood clearly outlined
against the dark cover of the easy-chair on
which he was resting. The bent head and
closed eyes indicated sleep, but this was con-
tradicted by frequent changes in the expression of his countenance. There was an air of
happiness, even of bliss, in his features; some
happy dream played about him like a golden
butterfly and dissolved every marked trait into
an expression of indefinite softness. Having
scanned the appearance of the sleeper for a
while Augustinowicz sat up in bed and viewed
his comrade with a feeling of indignation, even
of anger.

"What is up there?" whispered he. "You
even seem to deceive yourself.—Indeed, I

shall take upon myself to awaken him. Such a fellow!—Bless me, if I don't throw the pillow at him and crush the lamp,—wait!"—In a moment the necessary preparations were made; he placed himself in the most suitable position for carrying into effect the proposed bombardment,—but suddenly dropped down into his former position and drew the cover close to his chin.

Schwarz had opened his eyes.

"I wonder what he'll do," said Augustinowicz to himself while feigning to be soundly asleep.

His astonishment grew into positive fear, however, when Schwarz glanced about, not unlike a villain on the point of committing some foul deed, and opened a drawer in his desk, rummaging its contents.

"Bless me, the man is on the point of shooting himself or taking poison," soliloquized Augustinowicz.

Schwarz did not, however, entertain any thought of committing suicide by bullet or

18

poison. The article that he finally produced from the contents of the drawer was merely a glove;—a small yellowish, crumpled glove; a memento of no great significance, yet a historical gift of the kind that is accompanied by such words as *"Addio, caro mio!* Remember me!"—Schwarz was probably placed in a position similar to that of Delorges, who obtained a like treasure by going

> "Despite the lion and tiger as well
>   straight ahead.—"

Another problem was, however, whether he

> "left the lady sweet and fair."

The different generations of mankind are, as a rule, likely to agree better in foolish than in wise matters.—Schwarz pressed the glove to his lips.

"For sha—a—ame, old man!" roared Augustinowicz.

Joseph was deeply humiliated. Reflecting upon the matter afterward, he felt a keen sense of shame. Next morning he was gone before daybreak in order to avoid the presence of his friend who was still as indignant and angry as before.   Augustinowicz never expected to be so greatly disappointed in his views of a man. —"He is like all the rest," said he.   The thought created a feeling of aversion not unknown to those who have had similar experience and have been compelled to give up their favorable thoughts of some one hitherto immaculate person of their close acquaintance. The most important point appeared to be, however, that Schwarz was evidently thinking of renewing his relations to Lula.—"She will either die or become entirely insane," said he, referring to the widow Potkansky, "and I wish for her death most heartily.   Nothing could be more opportune."—He tried his utmost to persuade himself that he was a sincere womanhater.—"Schwarz will return, like a penitent sinner."—Having reflected thoroughly upon the matter he decided not to tell Lula that Schwarz intended marrying.

"I don't care much about Helen.—Well,

Joseph will return to Lula, but suppose I should tell everything, then it would be too late.   Upon my word!—And if I should go and tell Helen, the soup will be spilled there, too.   In that way I would avoid assisting the one and spoil matters with the other.   No, I shall keep quiet.   Silence is gold."

Augustinowicz preferrred Helen to Lula in every point of view and was most decidedly in favor of a marriage between Schwarz and Helen; but Joseph's welfare went before everything else, and he was ready to sacrifice every other consideration before that of Joseph's welfare.   For this reason he desired that Lula should remain free and hoped most sincerely that she would encourage Pelsky. — — "Then I shall say to the old man: Look here, I have said nothing whatever of Helen; Lula never learned that you loved the widow, and yet she will be married to Pelsky. And finally, he preserved the news of Helen's intended marriage until the hour when Lula had reached Pelsky her hand in marriage and thought no more of

Schwarz: — — "Then I shall go and tell the young couple that Schwarz presents his compliments; *crescite et multiplicamini!* He has long been engaged to marry a lady whom he loves. and who adores him:—the deuce!"

CHAPTER XVIII.

One day passed after another, and Schwarz appeared to think no more of returning to Lula.   Malinka said, however, to Augustino-wicz:

"Pelsky will speak to Lula to-day or to-morrow."

"And unless he does that, some day she, herself, will speak to him, I suppose."

"Oh, you are doing her great injustice!"

"We shall see."

"No, Pan Adam.   Lula is too proud for such things, and if she ever will marry Pelsky it will be the result of wounded pride; of anger on account of your friend's indifference. Otherwise, it is true that she loves no one if not Pelsky.   Of all men he remained alone true to her, and she can count on no one else."

"Ah, you think she is doing a certain amount of calculation?"

Malinka grew eager.

"One time she might be said, in a certain sense, to count on Schwarz,—and was disappointed.   Who will blame her for thinking no more of the man who never appears;—you understand me?—who never puts in appearance?"

Augustinowicz made no reply.

"She was bitterly disappointed," continued Malinka, "and probably no one but she and myself know how great that disappointment really was.   Although we are no more as intimate as before;—she, herself, has withdrawn —I see plainly how much she suffers.   Yesterday, on entering her room, I found her in tears —'Lula,' said I,—although I am not anxious to intrude,—'what gives you trouble?'—She answered that it was headache.   I wanted to take her in my arms, but she pushed me softly aside, and arose with such an expression of pride that I was nearly frightened.—'I wept for shame,' said she with emphasis,—'you understand me: For shame!'—I did not understand her altogether, but in the evening she was again weeping;—there, you see."

"What does it all signify?"

"It proves that she cannot easily give up all thoughts of Schwarz.—But what has happened?   Why does he never come here?"

"What if he did return?"

"In that case she would dismiss Pelsky at once."

"How ridiculous!—Dismiss him."

"You amuse yourself over everything.—Do you really think Schwarz is doing right in leaving her without an explanation?"

"Who knows what he thinks?"

"He ought to know better," declared Malinka, "at any rate, why should he make a secret of what he is doing?"

"He is very busy;—he is working."

On the very same day Malinka happened to notice, however, that Schwarz was not quite as busily engaged as Augustinowicz had implied.   She walked about the streets with her mother, and they met him in one of the thor-

oughfares, where he walked along, accompanied by another young man.   Although he
failed to recognize the two ladies, Malinka
was at once struck by his appearance.   He
was as pale and haggard as one just recovered
from a serious illness:—"Then, he must have
been sick," said the girl to herself.   Now she
understood why Augustinowicz refused to
state the reason of Joseph's continued absence:
Schwarz forbid him telling, in order not to
cause Lula any distress.   Thus Malinka came
to regard him in an ideal light.

In the evening Augustinowicz put in appearance as usual.

"I learned to-day," cried Malinka, "the reason why Herr Schwarz has not been here so
long."

Lula's eyes gleamed, and she was almost
unable to control herself.

"The poor young man!" interposed Madame Witzberg.   "He must have gone through
some serious illness.   Why did you never tell
us of his sickness?"

"I know the reason," said Malinka. "You were anxious to keep the matter from Lula. Was that fair and just to us?—What is the matter, Lula? Are you—?"

"Nothing, nothing! Only excuse me for a short while."

Her face was pale as death, and her breath was heavy. She left, or almost fled, from the room. Madame Witzberg arose to follow her, but Malinka prevented it by a gentle, but determined pressure on the old lady's arm.

"She needs no assistance, Mama, dear."

Turning to Augustinowicz she resumed, in an earnest, but sorrowful tone:

"Pan Adam!"

Augustinowicz bit his lips.

"Well, Pan Adam, do you still consider Lula a heartless flirt?—What do you say now?"

"I was really mistaken," stammered Augustinowicz, "but—but—"

He dared not tell her that Schwarz intended marrying Helen and would never return to Lula. Nor did he venture, after his return

home, breaking the news before Schwarz.
Lula had withdrawn to her room, a thousand thoughts making her heart aglow.
Schwarz, Pelsky, Malinka and Augustinowicz circled about her, and a dense fog began to obscure both Present and Future. Beyond it all was a vision of Joseph's countenance, deadly pale.

"He is ill, he is ill," said she to herself. He will die, and I shall never see him again."

Lula's theory of Joseph's absence was quite different from that of Malinka. She thought he had sacrificed himself to avoid standing between her own and Pelsky's happiness, and that he was now wasting his life away.—"Who told him that I should be happy in marrying Pelsky?" whispered she. "He did not trust me;— — oh, God, he did not trust me." Before her eyes floated a vision of moments when her pleasing smile and kind words were intended only for Pelsky, and she remembered with a blush of shame how she had resented the thought of Joseph being the son of a blacksmith. Even now she was blushing for shame, but the cause was a different one. In this moment she thought that even if Schwarz, himself, followed a blacksmith's trade she could think of no happier lot than being permitted to press her head against the black apron that might cover his broad chest.

"I never realized how much I love him," said she, quivering like in a state of fever.

For several days hence Augustinowicz did not appear, but in accordance with Malinka's prophecy Pelsky came and asked for his cousin's hand in marriage. Looking into the girl's face with its quiet, pleasant smile, he phrased his request as pompously as he knew, but was highly astonished at receiving a most emphatic refusal.

"I have given my heart to some one else," quietly confessed Lula.

Pelsky demanded to know who this person might be, and she told him frankly, offering— as it is customary—her friendship instead of the feeling that no more belonged to herself.

In taking leave Pelsky did not, however, accept even the proffered hand.

"You have taken too much from me, cousin," said he, "and offer me too little in return: Your friendship in return for a whole life's happiness!"

After his departure Lula gave no thought whatever to the reproach; her mind was occupied with matters of a totally different nature. The dark side of love is that one pays no attention to the consideration of others. Love is all-absorbing and excludes the regard due to individuals. The world about us, with the exception of the beloved one, might disappear without our realizing the slightest regret.

Such were Lula's thoughts when, having taken leave of Pelsky, she sought Malinka's presence and felt an irresistible desire of telling some one what had happened. Malinka was sitting at a window, seemingly absorbed in deep meditation. Suddenly she felt Lula's arms about her neck.

"Is it you, Lula?" asked the girl, softly.

"Yes, Malinka."

She seated herself on a foot-stool and laid her head in Malinka's lap.

"Malinka, dear, you are not angry with me. You do not despise me?"

Malinka stroked her hair.

"I know I was wrong, and that I acted in a sinful way. But now I have found my heart once more.—I like to be near you. Do you remember how many pleasant talks we had before?—Let us chat once more with each other. —Will you?"

Malinka smiled half sadly, half merrily, and replied:

"Probably we may do so yet, but not in the future. Before very long some one will come and rob me of Lula. Then I shall be alone."

"Will he come?" asked Lula.

"He will,—when he grows well again. At present he is sick and full of longing. I never understood why Pan Adam refused to say why he never appeared, but now I feel sure that

Schwarz forbid him;—he would cause you no trouble."

"And I thought he would not stand in the way of Pelsky."

"What did you answer Pelsky?"

"I was just now on the point of telling you: —to-day Pelsky asked me to become his wife."

"And you—?"

"I declined his offer."

A pause ensued.

"He would not even take my hand, when I bid him good-bye; but what else could I answer! I realize that he may have reasons for being angry with me;—and I was not right. But what else could I do, when I did not love him!"

"Better late than never. You followed the voice of your heart. You may yet become happy with Schwarz."

"Oh, yes, yes!"

"In a month hence," continued Malinka, "we shall dress our Lula all in white, and then she will be married to the man of her choice.

—Oh, he must be noble and good, since we all think so well of him."

"Yes,—all think so well of him," repeated Lula in laughter mingled with tears.

"We all do. Mama is even a little afraid of him,—and so am I," confessed the girl. "But I honor him with all my heart."

Lula placed both hands under her chin and reclined against Malinka, who fondled her in her arms with a happy smile. It had grown dark, and the moon rose. Outside was quiet, and within the room there was no sound except the whispering of the girls' voices.

Suddenly the sounding of the door-bell broke the silence.

"Probably it is he!" exclaimed Lula.

It was, however, not he, for the voice of Augustinowicz was a moment later heard in the hall:

"Are the ladies at home?"

"Lula, go into another room and hide yourself," said Malinka. "I'll tell him that you have declined Pelsky's offer; then he may go and tell Schwarz. Perhaps Schwarz will come at once, when he learns the truth."

Lula glided out of the room. A moment afterward the door was opened, and Augustin-owicz entered.

19

CHAPTER XIX.

It has already been mentioned that August-inowicz was not inclined to tell Schwarz what had happened at the Witzberg home. Lula fell short of his expectations, and loved the young physician in spite of Pelsky's continued attention. He gave the matter all his attention and involuntarily, in spite of her aristo-cratic demeanor, came to regard Lula with considerable respect.—Respecting a woman, as he did now for the first time, was so much out of proportion to his moral organization that he hardly knew what to think of himself. His feelings resembled those of a liar caught in some deceitful proceeding, and his idea of womanhood was the very lie in which he caught himself. His surprise was great. On some occasion now long forgotten the misan-thropic expression: "I wish there were some-where a perfect and noble woman, and that we

men were less superficial,"—had escaped him.
He avoided Schwarz, and even feared him, yet
always desired to tell him of the discovery he
had made regarding the Countess, but continued putting it off.   Finally Schwarz could not
avoid noticing his remarkable behavior.

"What is the matter, Adam?" asked he.

"Why not ask me outright?" cried Augustinowicz.   "Why not inquire about Lula?"

Schwarz started in great surprise.

"About Lula?—What do you mean?"

"Nothing whatever.—What could I mean?
—Is it necessary that everything should have
a certain significance?"

"Augustinowicz, you are trying to conceal
something."

"He is thinking of no one but Lula," cried
Augustinowicz in a state of almost complete
desperation.

Schwarz controlled himself, but not without
a great effort.   The aspect of his pale cheeks
and flashing eyes reminded one of the quiet before a storm.

"Now I'll tell you everything," exclaimed Augustinowicz, fearing an outbreak, "yes, everything. Who will prevent my speaking when you have won the play?—the deuce take me if you haven't. She loves you."

Schwarz was greatly agitated. A cold perspiration covered his forehead.

"And Pelsky—?" asked he.

"He said nothing to her as yet."

"Does she know everything about me?"

"Schwarz, let me—"

"Speak out!"

"She knows nothing whatever. I have told her nothing.'

There was a singular strain in Joseph's voice, as he continued:

"Why did you do that?"

"Schwarz, I thought you would return to her."

Joseph wrung his hands, until the joints were fairly creaking; Adam's last words touched him like burning coal.—Return to her?—Leave Helen forever, as though his very

conscience had not forbidden him such a step.
Returning to Lula implied happiness for all
days to come, but also the ruin, even the death
of Helen. He should become a man whose
sense of honor was lost forever,— a miserable
being who despised himself. The devil was already carrying on his satanic play within Joseph's soul; he realized where his inclinations
were carrying him. A host of thoughts, wishes and intentions arose in his mind; there was
a struggle everywhere.—Augustinowicz was
looking at his friend in a state of sheer desperation and felt a burning desire of seizing him
by the collar and kicking him from the room.
Suddenly Schwarz arose; a firm resolve was
written on his countenance. Some ball had
started rolling.

"Augustinowicz!"

"Well?"

"Go at once and tell Lula that I shall be
married in a month hence and will never return to her.—Understand me, never!"

Augustinowicz pulled himself together and

went. As we have already seen, he was received by Malinka. Behind the door of one of the adjoining rooms was Lula, who eagerly prepared herself listening to the proceedings of the two.

Malinka pressed Adam's hand with a kind smile, and Augustinowicz returned the pressure with genuine affection.

"I am pleased you came," said she. "We have a great deal—a very great deal—to talk about."

"I have, myself, much to say," replied Augustinowicz. "In fact, I appear before you in the capacity of an ambassador."

"From Schwarz?"

"From Schwarz!"

"Does he regain his health?"

"No,—still quite sick.—Was Pelsky here?"

"Yes, I was on the point of speaking about him."

"I listen, Miss Malinka."

"He has talked to Lula about marriage."

"Well.—and then?"

"She refused. Pan Adam, she loves only Schwarz, and will hear of no one but him,—the dear, brave Lula!"

A pause ensued. At length Augustinowicz began, in an unsteady tone:

"He will never marry her—"

"Pan Adam!"

"Schwarz has already pledged his word;—he will marry another woman."

The news struck the two girls like a thunderbolt. For several minutes there was a perfect silence in the room. Suddenly the door of one of the rooms adjoining the salon flew open and Lula entered. Her face aglow with wounded dignity, mingled with pride. She thought that everything sacred to her had been shamefully degraded.

"Malinka," said she, "I beseech you to ask no further questions. Enough has been said already. This gentleman has done his duty; why should we degrade ourselves by giving a reply?"

She seized Malinka's hand and drew the

girl, almost violently, from the room. Augustinowicz looked after them, shrugged his shoulders and said:

"By the Prophet, I understand her. She is right,—but so is Schwarz.—Well, I'd better strike while the iron is hot."

He left the house and went straight to Pelsky, giving him an account of the whole matter.

"A certain fatalism seems to rest upon both," concluded he.—"Schwarz could act in no other way. Am I not right?"

"He did exactly as he pleased, sir.—But, pray, tell me why you take the trouble to notify me of these things?"

"Oh, never mind! Permit me to ask if Lula did not act nobly in refusing your offer?"

"That is entirely immaterial. I prefer not to answer the question."

"Do as you please, my dear sir. It is immaterial to me in the way that I am not particularly interested in Lula. On the other hand, when Schwarz withdraws himself, her future life may hardly be enviable. You are closely related to her,—I am sorry — —

Pelsky grew pensive.

"You are sorry?—Why so?"

"I am sorry that you did not see fit to postpone your proposal."

The Count arose and measured the room with long steps.

"I shall never—" murmured he.

"Too late, too late, my dear sir," interposed Augustinowicz. "Permit me to ask you, however, that no one will learn from you that I paid you this visit,—particularly Schwarz and the Witzberg family."

"May I ask the reason?"

"It is very important, but you would not understand.—Good-bye."

Pelsky pondered long over this singular request on the part of Augustinowicz, but reached no intelligent conclusion. He was dimly conscious that it might concern himself in some way.

"I might return and affect to know nothing of it all," said he.—"Poor Lula!"

CHAPTER XX.

Malinka and Lula had retired to the room of the latter. Both maintained a painful silence. The poor Countess experienced some of the hardest moments of her whole life. Her holiest feelings seemed profaned beyond all hopes of reparation. The best elements of her moral existence were invested in this feeling of love, and victory had already seemed within her reach;—the very power of this love now raised her from the fall that seemed closely approaching, and induced her to decline the offer of a man who adored her,—to renounce a life in quietude, splendor and independence; — — and the outcome of it all was that he whom she loved had pledged his word to marry another woman!—But she had lost a great deal beside. Her pure, angelic serenity, the prominent characteristic of her former life, had given place to an overpowering sentiment of doubt.

Did she not lose, with her love, even the feeling of trust and hope that determined the whole extent of her material elements of life? The firm basis of her existence seemed to disappear, and she was placed in a position not unlike that of a boat deprived of its rudder. She, an orphan, was to-day guarded and fondled by loving hearts; to-morrow she might suffer the lot of the lonely;—to-day she was as pure as a lily, safe from all the troubles of bitterness,—a mere child, fresh as a morning in May; some future day might look upon her life's barren soil. Humiliated, bent like a tree before the tempest, deprived of her moral safety, her happiness killed by brutal hands, was she sitting there, holding Malinka close to her heart; with a blush upon her face, and large, tearless eyes. She could not weep; her anger was too great, but Malinka cried for them both.

———

Next morning the Countess received two

letters, one from Pelsky, another from Schwarz.

"Madam," wrote Pelsky. "The pain that was caused me by your unexpected reply did not permit me to choose my words as I should. I regret sincerely having refused the gift of your friendship. Even though I cannot explain your position toward me, I do not entertain the least doubt of your having obeyed the voice of your heart. May this voice not deceive you! If the man of your choice loves you as sincerely as I do, your happiness will be beyond doubt. I can entertain no aversion for the man of your choice and would never dare to criticize him. In my case, being forced to give up all hopes of possessing you, I ask you not to consider words uttered in a moment of pain and disappointment as an expression of my true feelings, and hope the valuable gift of your friendship will replace, to a certain extent, the happiness that cannot be mine."

Joseph's letter was brought by Augustino-wicz, and Lula refused to open it.

"Do not cause him this pain," said the young man. "The condition of my friend may at present be almost as—"

He suddenly stopped, overpowered, in spite of himself, by his feelings. After a short pause he continued: "Probably these may be his last words. Yesterday he was taken to the hospital."

Lula grew as pale as death and tried in vain to preserve her quiet and cool appearance. Her whole body trembled. In spite of everything she loved him still.—The letter contained the following:

"Although your course will be different from mine I cannot bear the idea that you despise me. So judge for yourself!—On his deathbed one of my friends entrusted to my care a woman whom he loved with all the strength of a disappointed and broken heart, and whose affection for him I gained without any step on my part. After his death I formed an acquaintance with her and thought her worthy of my love. In a weak moment I told her all.—The remainder is known to you. I tried to conceal my attachment to you before myself. My suffering was great, and I hope you will forgive me. I, too, am a human being who must attach myself to and gain the affection of, my fellow-beings. In words, I never made known that I loved you. At length, driven by the voice of conscience,—what could I do?—Where should I go, and how was I to choose? I promised my dead friend and pledged my word before the poor woman: Every consideration except that of my own heart bid me renounce you. It is not my fault that you failed to learn the truth until yesterday. You should have learned all when Pelsky first made his appearance. Through some unhappy mistake, everything went against the fulfilment of this plan.—This is a true statement of facts, and now you may judge for yourself,—and forgive me if you see fit. Adam has permitted you to think that I am sick; so it is: I cannot control my thoughts, and the heart is aglow within me; but through all pain and sorrow I see clearly that you alone are the woman whom I love."

Every trace of anger and wounded pride had disappeared from Lula's forehead and was followed by deep, hearty compassion.

"Pan Adam," said she to Augustinowicz. "Tell him that he could not have acted otherwise."

Augustinowicz bent his knees before her.

"You will also forgive me. I wronged you deeply in my thoughts. But how could I know that there was anywhere on earth a woman so noble and righteous!"

CHAPTER XXI.

Leaving the Witzberg home, Augustinowicz went straight to the hospital where he remained the whole night.   The condition of
Schwarz was very serious.   An attack of typhus was threatening to destroy his vigorous
body.   Towards midnight the patient began
manifesting signs of an approaching crisis,
talked to himself and plunged into a lively
discussion about the immortality of the soul
with a black cat that he imagined seeing at his
bedside.   Death seemed to frighten him greatly; more than once did Augustinowicz notice
a shadow of terror on his countenance.   He
was frightened at the touch of his friend;
sometimes he would sing songs, both amusing
and melancholy, or discuss different questions
with imaginary friends about him.   There was
a certain touching liveliness in the disjointed
fragments of speech that fell from his lips.

Augustinowicz, who had received a deep impression of the happenings of the last few days, was nearly beside himself with terror. Sitting at the bedside of his friend and benefactor he longed for the morning as never before and watched the progress of daybreak through the windows. The night was dark and rainy, and the splashing of the drops conveyed a monotonous and sombre sound to the narrow room. From time to time he would watch the features of the patient, and often he imagined noticing the touch of death on the pale countenance in the pillows.—Augustinowicz remembered the fact that this man, who had been hitherto as active and far-reaching as any, might be reduced, in a short while, to a dead mass that was buried in the ground, and —*finita la Comedia*. The end,—dust;—what a commonplace, invariably tiresome and awful idea to those who see nothing beyond. And yet, Joseph's life would have been even more active than that of most others.

The bitterness of these unpleasant thoughts

20

threw a dark shadow over Adam's forehead, and in the meantime the dark of the window panes changed into gray: The day was drawing near. Before the strong light of the east filled the room there was a general fading of the dim candles, and soon the steps of the hospital servants were heard outside. After having waited about an hour, Augustinowicz opened the door and was met on the threshold by the attending physician.

"What is the patient's condition?" inquired he.

"Poor, very poor," returned Augustinowicz, in a tone of deep concern.—The physician knit the brows, stepped forward and examined the pulse of the sufferer.

"What is your opinion?" asked he, turning again to Augustinowicz.

"My opinion?—Why, I have none;—he is ill, very ill."

"Well," observed the physician, "I hardly know what to say."

"I was just thinking, Doctor," pursued

Augustinowicz, "that the science of medicine has many features in common with the child that attempted to fly through the air by lifting its feet;—don't you think I am right?"

The physician made no reply, but shrugged his shoulders, prescribed certain antifebrile medicine and left the room. Augustinowicz glanced at the prescription, shrugged his shoulders in imitation of the medical attendant and resumed his seat at the bedside. Towards evening Joseph's condition grew worse, and by midnight he was almost dying. Augustinowicz wept like a child and struck his head against the wall. Toward morning he thought there was a slight change for the better, but this was only an illusion. The red and white spots characteristic of a certain variety of typhus commenced developing. During twilight Madame Witzberg called to inquire about Joseph's condition, but was not permitted entering the room. Adam's countenance bore an expression, however, that could not be mistaken. Fearing the worst, she exclaimed:

"Is he alive?"

"He will die," was the brief answer.

In a few hours the chaplain came and offered to administer the extreme unction to the sufferer, but Augustinowicz did not feel strong enough to witness the act. He felt the necessity of collecting himself. The poor fellow was prepared for anything but Joseph's death. Walking about the city in an aimless manner, he often stopped to consider if he might yet return in time,—and at length realized that he was standing before Helen's door.

"I'll walk in.—She must take leave of him."

Half an hour hence there was a woman kneeling at Joseph's bedside. Her hair floated down over both shoulders, and she was gazing intently on the patient's face. The room had long been perfectly quiet, except for the slow, oppressed breath of the dying man. Slowly, terribly slowly, did the long hours of darkness pass over the sick room. Every minute seemed to be the last moment of the patient's life.

At length the crisis was over, and a change for the better followed. Augustinowicz and Helen did not leave the bed except when it was necessary to the patient; both appeared to forget entirely the world about them. With the return of Joseph's vital force also came Helen's realization of the world about her; she rejoiced over every sign of progress. At length Schwarz regained consciousness. Augustinowicz happened to be absent, and the first figure upon whom Joseph's eyes rested was that of Helen. For a while he remained quietly glancing at her; it was evident that he attempted collecting his thoughts. At length he recognized her and smiled faintly. The smile was forced, however, even though Helen fell upon her knees and wept for joy. On his return Augustinowicz noticed that the presence of the young woman irritated the patient. Schwarz followed with his glance all her movements, and his lips and eyelids were quivering nervously. Augustinowicz watched his friend with some anxiety; he expected no good.—Towards evening the fever again grew severe, as is usual in such cases; the patient slumbered, and Augustinowicz attempted persuading Helen to return home and get the rest she highly needed.

"I cannot leave him even for a single moment," returned Helen with unusual emphasis.

Augustinowicz took his seat and plunged into deep meditation, but soon his head grew heavy and the eyelids seemed hard to lift. An irrepressible sleepiness took more and more possession of him. Before very long he was reclining in his chair and carried away into a dreamless stupor. With a start he awoke, some time later, and looked around in a state of bewilderment.

"Is he asleep?" asked he, motioning toward the patient.

"He is somewhat restless," whispered Helen.

Augustinowicz relapsed into his former attitude, but was suddenly aroused by a loud cry from Helen, and jumped to his feet. Schwarz was sitting up in bed, his face aglow with fever, his eyes gleaming like those of a wolf, stretching one thin arm towards Helen.

"What has happened?" cried Augustinowicz.

Helen threw her arms around the quivering figure of the man upon whom her own existence was wholly dependent.

"Don't choke me," whispered Joseph, in a rattling, unsteady tone. "You killed Gustave, and now you desire to kill me. — — Leave the room. —I—I do not love you."

He fell back among the pillows.

"Lula,—dear Lula, help me!" groaned he.

Augustinowicz led Helen from the room, almost by physical power. In the hall there was some hurried talking, and some one uttered the name of the Countess.

At length Augustinowicz returned to the sick room alone. He was pale, and large drops of perspiration were standing on his forehead.

"The matter is settled," whispered he.

———

Helen rushed out into the night, driven by despair. Joseph's words and her brief talk with Augustinowicz had touched, like a sudden flash of fire, many circumstances still unknown to her. She pursued her way through the streets in an aimless manner. Her thoughts burned like fire within her, or turned about her head like a burning, whirling mass. It was evening, and thousands of lights gleamed from the many windows, behind which peace and homeliness were dwelling; she pursued her way regardless of everything. The streets were filled with large streams of men and women, each bent upon a certain course; a great many by-passers glanced around after her. A young man even stopped and addressed some words to her with a smile.

but withdrew himself on seeing her face. She
left the streets and entered a narrow passage,
empty and dark; no lights appeared in the windows behind which the working families slept
after the exertions of the day; at long intervals there was a sound of steps or a streak of
light from some lonely lamp. The night was
dark and moist, and the air was heavy; a cold
wind blew from the banks of the Dneiper, and
the fog in the air clung to Helen's dress and
hair. In spite of the cold it seemed to her as
though the fire of heaven fell upon her head
and bosom and arms. Her shawl was lost in
the wind, and when her bonnet slipped off the
long tresses of dark hair fell down over her
shoulders and her back. More than once she
stumbled and fell, and soon was alone in the
dead of the night. The far-away noise from
the city and the barking of the dogs followed
her. She felt neither exhausted nor sorry;
all her thoughts gathered about the facts of
her hopeless fate. The disappointment she
had suffered frustrated all her hope of life

and Future; rest was to be found not in life, but in death. The incessant exertion deprived her entirely of her strength. Her lips grew dry, her eyes were dim, and her clothes soiled and wet. She rushed onward until hardly able to breathe.

The rushing of the water grew more and more audible. Helen stopped and listened to the singular, capricious murmur of the waves. A short while she stopped at the river bank. Then, with closed eyes and outstretched arms, she plunged forward. There was a sharp, wild cry, followed by a deep silence.

The night was blacker than ever.

CHAPTER XXII.

"Many singular transitions are taking place in this miserable world," says an old poet. It is certain, at least, that in many cases the thread of life becomes so entangled that certain questions must receive the same treatment as the Gordian knot. Such was the attitude in which Schwarz found himself. A few years before he had commenced his academic life with a strong conviction of his own power; at present it seemed as though his ability to promote the fate of others as well as that of himself had been exhausted, and that he was hardly able to govern the course of his own little boat. He soon realized that in future days the wind alone would guide his progress. The happiness he had hoped for was wasted. In his case, as well as in many others, the unruly life of youth had entered the too narrow channel of love, but the river bed was narrow, nence the torrent grew wild and noisy, and for that reason there were but few peaceful moments in Joseph's life. This stormy past came very near resulting in the total loss of his life,—certainly it was staking too much. The last scene with Helen seemed to increase the danger. Augustinowicz feared a relapse, but happily it failed to materialize, and Schwarz was improving day by day. The duration of his convalescence could not be determined, as he would remain weak for a considerable length of time. Augustinowicz did his best to shorten his long hours of tedious waiting, but in spite of his exertion Joseph's mood failed to grow brighter. The mental struggle to which he was still subjected rendered him earnest and unconversable. Augustinowicz, on his part, was greatly changed. Since the beginning of Joseph's sickness were his visits at the Witzberg residence discontinued, but the lady, herself, made frequent calls to ascertain the patient's condition.

If Augustinowicz had been influenced by

the incidents of the latter days, there was a
still greater change in Schwarz.

He arose from his sick-bed a different being: His lively, energetical, unflinching temper had left him entirely. The slow movements; the unwieldy glance; the weakness
were attributed by Augustinowicz to the effects of the illness, and would, thought he,
disappear after the time of convalescence, but
ere long there were other changes noticeable:
He seemed to be lost in a certain state of indifference, even of apathy. True, he began taking interest in the world about him, but from
a new point of view. He seemed totally foreign to any bright or lively feeling. It was
pitiful to notice how the change in him
touched both his moral and physical being:
He became bald-headed; the expression of
his countenance was haggard; the eyes were
dull and had lost all of their former lustre.
Resting in his bed one day after another he
glanced continually into one direction or
stared about the room in a vacant manner.

until the stupor of sleep closed his eyes. There seemed to be no one in whose presence he was especially interested.—All this troubled Augustinowicz considerably, and he sighed more than once at the thought of the former appearance of his friend, whose state of mind was evidently, if possible, even more hopeless than before.

One day Augustinowicz was sitting at the bedside of Joseph, reading aloud to him. The vacant stare of the patient indicated that his thoughts were far away from the subject in which the friend was anxious to awaken his interest. As Augustinowicz noticed a tired expression on his countenance, he stopped reading and asked:

"Would you rather sleep, old man?"

"No, but the book tires me."

Augustinowicz had been reading the *Dame aux Camelias.*

"Yet it abounds in life and truth, my friend."

"I admit that,—but not a grain of intelligent judgment."

"Well, but the book treats of the fate of such women as—"

"What do such women concern me?"

"Sometime they did!"

Schwarz made no reply, but assumed a pensive air.—In a little while he resumed:

"What do you know of Helen?—Was she not here?"

"Certainly, old man, certainly—" returned Augustinowicz, who was unable to conceal his embarrassment.

"Well, and where is she at present?"

"At present she is ill,—very, very ill."

Schwarz remained perfectly indifferent.

"How so?" inquired he, in a lazy tone.

"The illness, oh,— — Well, I'd rather tell you the plain truth, only don't become excited."

"Well?"

"Helen is no more alive;—she was drowned."

A faint quiver passed over Joseph's face, and he attempted sitting up in bed, but finally leaned back among the pillows.

"Accidentally or—wilfully?" asked he.

"Rest yourself, old man, rest yourself. Remember that you are not allowed to do much talking yet. Some time I shall tell you everything."

Schwarz turned his face towards the wall and remained perfectly quiet.—A servant opened the door and said to Augustinowicz:

"Madame Witzberg is here and would like to speak to you."

Augustinowicz stepped out into the hall, where the lady was waiting.

"What has happened?" asked he. "Has something occurred?"

"No, no;—yes—"

"Anything important?"

"Lula has left us," returned the old lady, in a tone of great concern.

"Long ago?"

"Last night.—Even if that had not happened I would have called here, since we received no news about Schwarz, and Malinka has wept so much and was in such a condition that I hardly dared leave her alone.—Lula has left us."

"For what reason?"

"Let me tell you: About two weeks after Herr Schwarz took sick we received another visit from Pelsky, and soon afterward he renewed his offer to Lula. It gave her great pain, as the poor young man loved her most sincerely. She refused, however, saying that she could not think of marriage without love. —I admired Pelsky highly, but that does not belong here. It is enough to say that the dear, brave girl refused his offer a second time. How much she suffered on account of your friend's illness!—Her parting from Pelsky was in every way a friendly one, and the young man obtained some commission, necessitating an immediate journey to Odessa. Imagine my surprise when a few days ago she came and told me that nothing but your friend's

21

illness had delayed her departure from our house, but as Schwarz was at present beyond all possible danger she would no longer be a burden to us, but earn her bread somewhere else. Oh, gracious heaven, as if she had ever been a burden to me! Malinka has profited greatly by associating with her and has improved her manners more than I expected, but otherwise I was as proud of her as if she had been my own daughter."

The poor old lady was deeply moved. After a long pause, Augustinowicz replied:

"No, my dear Madame! I understand why Lula took that step. When she consented to remain at your house, she was yet a spoiled, capricious child, and thought you desired her company on account of her coronet and the splendor that it might impart to your house.— Now it is all different."

"Did I ever reproach her—?" interrupted Madame Witzberg.

"That is of no consequence. I comprehend how difficult it may be to you to witness her departure and wish you had told me of her intentions before her departure.—The woman whom Schwarz was to marry is no more."

"Is no more?"

"Exactly.—But regardless of the trouble on your part, there is no particular reason to regret what has happened. Schwarz must yet possess his doctor's degree, as it is necessary to his future existence. When his health is restored, and he has gained some position in the world, he may seek her at Odessa or elsewhere;—but that will require some time. Schwarz is greatly changed, and Lula's decision, which may only tend to increase his affection for her, will work no harm."

Madame Witzberg left the building much depressed. Augustinowicz pondered a little before returning to the sick-room; at length he said to himself:

"She refused Pelsky's offer a second time; — — she will earn her bread! — — Ah, Schwarz, Schwarz, Schwarz! To win such a woman even through greater sufferings — —"

He did not finish the thought, but stepped back into the sick-room.

"What was Madame Witzberg's errand?" inquired Schwarz carelessly.

"Lula has left her," replied Augustinowicz.

Schwarz closed his eyes and remained immovable for some time.   At length he exclaimed:

"I am sorry.—Lula was a dear child."

Augustinowicz bit his lips, but said nothing.

———

Schwarz left the hospital in due course, and was graduated a month hence. The two friends returned home on a beautiful autumn day with their respective diplomas. Joseph's countenance was yet marked by the serious illness he had undergone, otherwise his body had recovered to a great extent from the effects thereof; Augustinowicz had taken hold of his arm and began talking of the past.

"Let us be seated on this bench," said Augustinowicz, as they passed through the public gardens. "What a splendid day! I always like to bathe myself in autumn sunshine."

They were seated.—Augustinowicz drew a long breath, stretched his limbs and said in a tone of genuine satisfaction:

"Well, old man! Three months ago we should have received these documents, if Fate had served us right."

"To be sure,—and now fall has come," returned Schwarz, rattling with his cane among the withered leaves on the ground.

"Yes, the leaves are falling, and the birds begin turning toward the South," said Augustinowicz, adding, with reference to a flock of goldfinches high up in the tree-tops,— "Will you not follow the course of those tiny messengers."

"I?—Where should I go?"

"To the Black Sea,—to Odessa."

Schwarz remained quiet for a while, and when at length he met the glance of his friend there was a mark of despair on his countenance.

"Adam," whispered he, "I love her no more."

In the evening, Augustinowicz said to Schwarz:

"We are wasting too much of our power in the pursuit of woman's love. Love flies from us like a swift bird, and our vitality is shattered."

THE END.